Alexander Thomson

**Whist, a Poem in Twelve Cantos**

Alexander Thomson

**Whist,  a Poem in Twelve Cantos**

ISBN/EAN: 9783744716222

Printed in Europe, USA, Canada, Australia, Japan

Cover: Foto ©Andreas Hilbeck / pixelio.de

More available books at **www.hansebooks.com**

# WHIST:

## A

## POEM,

### IN

## TWELVE CANTOS.

——————Ridentem dicere verum

Quid vetat?——————            HORACE.

*L O N D O N:*

PRINTED FOR J. AND B. BELL, NO. 148, OXFORD-STREET;

E. HARLOW, ST. JAMES'S-STREET; AND

C. FORSTER, IN THE POULTRY.

M DCC XCI.

# ADVERTISEMENT.

*IT was suggested to the author of the following perform-ance, that it would be proper to enter a caution with his readers, to prevent any unfavourable impression, which some of the sentiments that occur in the work might possibly leave upon the minds of those to whom he has the honour of being personally known. This however was a species of liberty which he could not by any means be persuaded to take ; as he could not suppose any one of his readers endowed with so small a degree of penetration, as not to perceive that most of the sentiments were introduced by him merely in support of the character which, for the sake of embellishment, he thought proper to assume—the character of a vain, petulant stripling, whose opinion of his own wit and abilities is so overweening, that he thinks they entitle him to fall foul of every thing that comes in his way.*

A MASK, SAYS CASTIGLIONE, CONFERS A RIGHT
OF SPEAKING AND ACTING WITH LESS RESTRAINT,
EVEN WHEN THE WEARER HAPPENS TO BE KNOWN.
JOHNSON.

# W H I S T.

## CANTO I.

# ARGUMENT.

Folly of writing on unfafhionable fubjects.—Several fa-

fhionable ones propofed.—Whift chofen.—Plan of the

work, and invocation to the fpirit of Hoyle.

Cofa non detta in *Blank-Verfo*, ne'n Rima.

ARIOSTO.

LET vulgar bards fome lofty fubject chufe,
And court a dull, unfafhionable Mufe,
In fruitlefs labour wafte their weary days,
Nor folid pudding gain, nor empty praife—
Let them for tragic numbers rack their brains,  5
And foar to all the pomp of epic ftrains—
Fools that they are! to think their filly art
Can thaw the winter of a modern heart;
To think that thofe at fancied griefs will cry
Whofe deareft friend might drop without a figh;  10
That thofe, whofe ev'ry ftep from felf proceeds,
Will read with pleafure of heroic deeds,

Virtues admire which never ftruck their view,
And feel for paffions which they never knew.

  Let others vainly ftrive to mend the times,  15
By lafhing follies, and expofing crimes:

While

While I, feduc'd by no fuch idle rage,

Turn to account the foibles of the age ;

Each reigning tafte with approbation feed,

And nothing write, but what the world may read. 20

Fain would I try fome fafhionable ftrain,

And fing the glories of NEWMARKET's plain ;

Shew by what arts the well-defcended horfe

Is train'd, and fed, and fitted for the courfe ;

And paint the tumults of each jockey's foul,     25

When all the panting fteeds approach the goal ;

When now the riders' heels their fides explore,

And all the verdant turf is ftain'd with gore ;

While each with double force the fcourge applies,

And fhame or triumph in one moment lies.     30

Or with what pleafure could the modifh Mufe

Her brighteft pow'rs and nobleft efforts ufe,

In praife of him who firft, with happy fkill,

* Improv'd the crefted bird of clarion fhrill,

---

The cock's fhrill clarion, or the echoing horn.
                              GRAY's ELEGY.

With

With more than nature's weapons arm'd his rage, 35
Taught him to death the bloody war to wage;
And made what once was but a dunghill fight
A strife which Dukes can witnefs with delight!
　　Or, higher still my daring voice to raife,
Shall I attempt th' illustrious boxer's praife;      40
Defcribe the show'r of thick tempestuous blows,
Which on the foe his heavy hand bestows;
And paint the rapture of th' admiring crowd,
Their eager joy, and acclamations loud,
When, at the last, he knocks him fairly down,     45
For England's glory, and his own renown,
And fends him bleeding from the noble fray,
With batter'd bones and skinlefs front away?
　　This could I do, the bold but lucky strain
In time, perhaps, might royal notice gain;        50
And fome bright year, the future years among,
With laureat honours might reward the fong.
　　But themes like thefe (tho' none could better chufe)
Are much too arduous for my humble Mufe;

　　　　　　　　　　　　　　　　　Who

Who dares not truſt her young unpractis'd wings  55
To ſoar the height of ſuch majeſtic things.

An art there is, of univerſal fame,
Which he who treats may public honours claim ;
That fav'ry art which teaches how to live,
To ev'ry diſh its proper ſauce to give,                60
Inſtructs to boil, to roaſt, and fricaſſee,
And callipaſh compoſe, and callipee :
All too with which the earth and ample ſkies,
Or liquid world, the board of man ſupplies,
This noble art directs us how to uſe,                 65
And Indian Curry make, and French ragouts.
But e'en this taſk my caution muſt decline,
And leave to talents better tried than mine.

One theme remains, which, could I treat it well,
Might gain me credit, and perhaps might ſell—  70
A ſober theme, which yet the young and gay
Would ſcarce be mov'd to toſs with ſcorn away.
A game I mean—that grave, judicious game,
Which took, as all agree, its warning name

From that ſtrict ſilence which its rules demand    75
From all that play, or near the players ſtand.
To ſuch a theme, the 'prentice and the peer,
Her grace and Betty, all would lend an ear;
For ſcarce one Briton, or one Briton's wife
Exiſts within the pale of ſocial life,                  80
But plays ſuch game as gameſters reckon good,
Or thinks he can, or wiſhes that he could.—
Nor in thoſe domes of wide-extended fame,
Which bear or White's, or Brookes', or Boodle's
         name,
(Where knights, and beaux, and lords, and ſharpers
         run,                                          85
Some to undo, but more to be undone;
Where all is huſh'd in trembling hope around,
And not one tongue emits an idle ſound)
Is this nice game (tho' higher bets are laid)
With deeper thought, or keener ardor play'd,    90
Than in the village alehouſe, where the door
Opes with a latch, and ſand beſtrews the floor;

                                              And

And where th' exciseman lank, of brow severe;

The priest, whose cure is twenty **pounds** a-year;

The farmer grave, in drugget coarse array'd;    95

And the gay miller, whiten'd by his trade,

Each ev'ning meet, to join in warm debate,

To drink hot punch, and regulate the state,

Some pence to stake, and o'er their pipes to risk

Th' uncertain issue of a game at Whisk.    100

 WHIST, then, delightful WHIST, my theme shall

  be,

And first I'll try to trace its pedigree,

And shew what sage and comprehensive mind

Gave to the world a pleasure so refin'd:

Then shall the verse its various charms display,    105

Which bear from ev'ry game the palm away;

And, last of all, those rules and maxims tell,

Which give the envied pow'r to play it well.

 But first (for such the mode) some tuneful shade

Must be invok'd, the vent'rous Muse to aid.    110

        Cremona's

Cremona's poet fhall I firft addrefs,

Who paints with fkill the mimic war of chefs,

* And India's art in Roman accents fings ;

Or him who foars on far fublimer wings,

Belinda's bard, who taught his liquid lay 115

† At Ombre's ftudious game fo well to play ?

But why thus vainly hefitates the Mufe,

In idle doubt, what guardian pow'r to chufe ?

What pow'r fo well can aid her daring toil,

As the bright fpirit of immortal Hoyle ? 120

By whofe enlighten'd efforts Whift became

A fober, ferious, fcientific game ;

To whofe unwearied pains, while here below,

The great, th' important privilege we owe,

That random ftrokes difgrace our play no more, 125

But fkill prefides, where all was chance before.

Come then, my friend, my teacher, and my guide,

Where'er thy fhadowy ghoft may now refide ;

* Marci Hieronymi Vidæ Scacchia, Ludus.
† Vide Pope's Rape of the Lock, c. iii. 25—100.

Perhaps

Perhaps (for Nature ev'ry change defies,

Nor ev'n with death our ruling paſſion dies)      130

With fond regret it hovers ſtill, unſeen,

Around the tempting boards array'd in green;

Still with delight its fav'rite game regards,

\* And, tho' it plays no more, o'erlooks the cards.

 Come then, thou glory of Britannia's iſle,      135

On this attempt propitious deign to ſmile;

Let all thy ſkill th' unerring page inſpire,

And all thy zeal my raptur'd boſom fire:

So ſhall I not diſgrace my theme ſublime,

Untouch'd as yet in each poetic clime,      140

In free unfetter'd verſe, or more melodiousrhime.

---

 \* And, tho' ſhe plays no more, o'erlooks the cards.

       RAPE OF THE LOCK.

# WHIST.

## CANTO II.

## ARGUMENT.

Introductory reflections on the invention of Cards—
Difficulty of discovering the inventor of Whist—
Story of Moody and his two Aunts.

HOW oft, in this capricious fcene of things,

Extenfive good from partial evil fprings;

And that for which whole kingdoms now may mourn

A bleffing proves to nations yet unborn !

When frenzy's pow'r the Gallic monarch * feiz'd, 5

Derang'd his thoughts, and all his mind difeas'd,

Unhappy France contending factions tore,

† And drench'd her meadows and her ftreets in

gore :

* Charles VI.

† On fe battait dans les rues, dans les églifes, dans les mai-
fons, à la campagne.

VOLTAIRE, ESSAI SUR L'HIST. GEN. ch. lxxix.

By

By turns fhe fuffer'd from the fierce alarms
Of feuds domeftic, and of foreign arms;          10
And all-defencelefs left, an eafy prey
To our wild Hal's awaken'd fpirit lay.

But had this haplefs prince efcap'd the fpleen,
How difmal now had our condition been !
Had med'cine's aid his fell diftemper cur'd,          15
What man of tafte could now have life endur'd ?
Poffeft of no refource, no art fublime,
To banifh thought, and kill the tedious time,
* How oft, like Job, would he have curs'd his day,
And idly yawn'd the liftlefs hours away !          20
But chief when fabbath comes with tirefome reft
To vulgar fouls, by weekly toils oppreft ;
When cruel cuftom fhuts amufement's door,
And dancers fkip, and fingers fqueak no more ;
What languor then had all our nerves unftrung, 25
And o'er each modifh houfe what vapours hung !

---

* Ahri ken, pethah Ayub ath piéu, vikillal ath Jumu.
                         JOB, ch. iii. 1.

But

But now the world is quite another thing,

Thanks to the madnefs of the Gallic king ;

Which, tho' the caufe of temporary ftrife,

Produc'd the brighteft charm of modern life.    ' 30

Some courtly fage, in that aufpicious hour,

Infpir'd by wifdom's philanthropic pow'r,

To cheer the darknefs of his monarch's mind,

Some new, unbroach'd delight effay'd to find ;

\* And then to light that fair quaternion fprung, 35 &#125;

O'er which both high and low, both old and young, &#125;

Have fince, thro' ev'ry age, in rapture hung ;    &#125;

Thofe pow'rful Clubs, which, ev'n when us'd in
    town,

Can ftrike, at times, a rural manfion down ;

Thofe fatal Spades, which, wielded by a knave,    40

Have dug for fome poor fools an early grave ;

\*——Elements, the eldeft birth
Of nature's womb, that in quaternion run,
Perpetual circle, multiform.

MILTON's PAR. LOST, v. 180.

B 2                    Diamonds,

Diamonds, which fcarce with lefs attraction fhine
Than thofe that glitter in Golconda's mine ;
And flaming Hearts, which glow with am'rous fire,
And love unfeign'd in ev'ry breaft infpire.            45
Then firft thofe wondrous forms arofe to view,
The fame for ever, yet for ever new ;
Thofe Kings in party-colour'd pomp array'd,
Who now fo long have Europe's fceptre fway'd ;
Thofe Queens, whofe charms, fuperior to decline, 50
Four ages paft, with equal glory fhine ;
Thofe who, in fraud's acknowledg'd liv'ry dreft,
Like other Knaves, are not the lefs careft :
And, each in order due—th' inferior train,
Which paint with red and black the verdant plain ; 55
That fpotted train, whofe amicable ftrife
With brilliant hues diverfifies our life.

But men had long thefe nobleft books perus'd,
And long with various games their hours amus'd,
Ere Whift appear'd, the charm of ev'ry heart,    60
The laft beft effort of inventive art.

                                        Let

\* Let India vaunt her children's vaſt addreſs,
Who firſt contriv'd the warlike † ſport of Cheſs;
Let nice Picquette the boaſt of France remain,
And ſtudious Ombre be the pride of Spain;    65
Invention's praiſe ſhall England yield to none,
While ſhe can call delightful Whiſt her own.

But to what name we this diſtinction owe,
Is not ſo eaſy for us now to know:
The Britiſh annals all are ſilent here,    70
Nor deign one friendly hint our doubts to clear:
Ev'n Hume himſelf, whoſe philoſophic mind
Could not but love a paſtime ſo refin'd;

---

\* Telle fut la manière d'écrire des Indiens. Leur eſprit
paraît encore davantage dans les jeux de leur invention. Le
jeu que nous appellons les Echecs, par corruption, fut inventé
par eux; et nous n'avons rien qui en approche; il eſt allégo-
rique comme leurs fables; c'eſt l'image de la guerre.
     VOLTAIRE, ESSAI SUR L'HIST. GEN. ch. iii.

† Ludimus effigiem belli, ſimulataque veris
Prælia————     VIDÆ SCACCHIA, I.

Ungrateful

Ungrateful Hume, who till his dying day
Continued still his fav'rite game to play* ;          75
Tho' many a curious fact his page supplies,
To this important point a place denies.

   Here might some bards unlock their classic store,
And deck their verse with mythologic lore ;
To wisdom's Queen th' invention might assign,          80
Or Jove himself, or ev'n the tuneful Nine.
But I should scorn my readers to deceive,
Or tell them aught but what they could believe :
And now, alas ! the whole Olympian state
Has lost its credit, and is out of date ;          85
Our wits, to whom their names are quite a bore,
Would only skip such pretty stories o'er :

   Upon his return to Edinburgh, though he found himself
weaker, yet his cheerfulness never abated ; and he continued to
divert himself, as usual, with correcting his own works for a
new edition, with reading books of amusement, with the con-
versation of his friends ; and sometimes, in the evening, with
a party at his favourite game of whist.
      LETTER FROM DR. SMITH TO WILL. STRAHAN.

For

For which good caufe no borrow'd light divine
Shall gild this round unvarnifh'd tale of mine;
In which the doubtful voice of vague renown          90
The likely Sire of Whift has handed down;
Which o'er its birth a glimm'ring luftre throws,
Nor tells, but rather gueffes how it rofe.

   A Yorkfhire dame invok'd the midwife's care,
And bleft her hufband with a fon and heir.          95
His infant frame appear'd robuft enough,
But fcarcely made of penetrable ftuff:
Nor bitter fquall, nor whimper deep and low,
Announc'd his entrance on the ftage of woe.
When on his face the facred fluid fell,             100
No cry efcap'd, his fad furprife to tell.
With rattling toys he ftill refus'd to play,
* And from his coral tore the bells away.

* I threw away my rattle before I was two months old; and
would not make ufe of my coral, till they had taken away the
bells from it.                              SPECTATOR, No. 1.

B 4                                              When

When loud or piercing founds affail'd his ear,

Each look betray'd his horror and his fear :          105

But chief he feem'd to dread the ftrife of tongues ;

For then alone he ftrain'd his little lungs,

And with a rueful face inceffant roar'd,

Till the ftorm ceas'd, and filence was reftor'd.

Hard was the tafk and wearifome, to teach          110

His backward tongue the mimic art of fpeech ;

Nor, when at laft your patience won the day,

Did he, like other babes, your care repay.

Ne'er did his prattle charm a parent's ear ;

He fcarcely utter'd twenty words a year.          115

Oft would he fly to fome fequefter'd nook,

To pore in quiet o'er a pictur'd book ;

Or fit whole hours immers'd in thought profound,

With eyes that fondly lov'd the fenfelefs ground ;

Till nature's wants, from which no frame is free, 120

Rous'd the young Stoic from his reverie.

To fchool for once he went ; but threat nor pray'r

Could force his feet again to venture there ;

Not

Not that, like fome, his tafk had wrought him woe
(His wit was quick, altho' his tongue was flow); 125
Nor that he fear'd the mafter's awful nod
(Th' attentive fcholar feldom dreads the rod) :
His fear was only from the boift'rous noife
Rais'd by fo many wild unruly boys :
Their favage tumult tore his tender ear, 130
Diftreft him more than what his frame could bear;
And, had his parents forc'd him ftill to go,
Might foon have fent him to the fhades below.

A grave and fober tutor next was found,
To lead him foftly thro' the claffic ground. 135
One charge there was he never would obey—
A tafk of any length aloud to fay :
The yielding tutor took it written down ;
But then he feldom read it with a frown.

His parents thus, of temper foft and mild, 140
In all his freaks indulg'd their wayward child ;
Not without hope that gravity fo young,
Such love of filence, fuch command of tongue,

When

When the wild feafon of caprice was paft,
Would furely rife to fomething great at laft— 145
A judge perhaps, of ftern fevere renown ;
Perhaps a bifhop, dreft in hallow'd gown ;
Or at the worft a mayor in fome adjacent town.

 When twice nine years had thus **at home been**
   fpent,
The grave young Moody was to **Cambridge** fent ; 150
Where, led by **no** temptation's pow'r aftray,
He pafs'd the time in his accuftom'd **way ;**
Seldom abroad, or in the common hall,
Read much, heard little, and fpoke none **at all.**

 But now ftern fate his father call'd away,   155
**And fent him** home, impatient to allay
Maternal anguifh for a lofs fo great,
And take poffeffion of his own eftate ;
In which he hop'd, remote from noife and ftrife,
To pafs in peace profound his future **life—**   160
**Peace,** the dear idol of his ftoic mind,
Which ev'n in Cam's retreats he could not find ;

         For

For there some youths, who felt a barb'rous joy
Their graver neighbour's comfort to destroy,
Each art employ'd that to their fancies rose,          165
His ears to wound, and murder his repose.

At home arriv'd, his father's widow'd mate
With transport sprung, to meet him at the gate;
But not alone—with her two virgins came,
Who long had kept that venerable name;          170
For fluent tongues o'er all the country fam'd.
They both to him an aunt's relation claim'd.
But who can tell with what unruly joy
They welcom'd home the long-departed boy;
From ev'ry mouth what floods of kindness broke;          175
How all at once with eager fury spoke;
How each by turns to raise their voices tried;
How much was ask'd; how little was replied!
The youth, in chains of mute amazement bound,
And almost deafen'd by the mighty sound,          180
With patience yet the rousing larum bore,
In hopes its violence would soon be o'er;

And

And that the dames, before the close of day,

Would kindly take their eloquence away.

Impatient oft he call'd the friendly night,          185

\* And oft with pleasure view'd the failing light:

But, oh, how killing was his sad surprise,

How much of horror fill'd his gloomy eyes;

What looks of dumb despair to heav'n were cast,

When, after waiting long, he found at last          190

That both were doom'd, by fate's perverse decree,

Perpetual inmates of the house to be;

Call'd by their sister, when she lost her mate,

To soothe her sorrows with their charming prate!

With such fair prospects op'ning to his view,          195

What now, alas, could luckless Moody do?

How dire the thought, that each succeeding day

In such a whirlwind must be pass'd away!

Ev'n from his inmost soul the mourner sigh'd;

Low sunk his heart, and all his courage died.          200

---

\* Polla pros Æelion kephalèn trepe pamphaneênta,
  Dûnai epeigomenos.

                    HOMER's ODYSSEY, Xiii. 29.

                                        But

But ftill refolv'd to fnatch from vocal ftrife

Whate'er his wayward fate allow'd of life,

A mind he feign'd on ftudious thoughts intent,

Each morning duly to his chamber went,

And there the precious hours with filence fpent. 205

But no excufe could fave the clofing day

From always paffing in a focial way :

His own politenefs could not this refufe,

Nor yet fo ill his mother's fifters ufe.

Then rofe the ftorm ; but ere its rage was o'er, 210

And left thy bark on midnight's quiet fhore,

How much, ill-fated youth, thy patience bore !

And oft affail'd at once by all the three,

* Thy deareft foe might fure have pitied thee.

One had a fcheme to better his eftate, 215

And one advis'd him how to chufe a mate ;

The third, determin'd not to be outdone,

Would kindly teach him how to rear his fon.

---

* Would I had met my deareft foe in heav'n.
                    SHAKESPEAR's HAMLET, Act 1, Sc. 4.

Then

Then enter'd fell Debate, with angry face ;

Each eager tongue assum'd a quicker pace,    220

And Peace affrighted rose, and fled the dang'rous
    place.

A short-liv'd calm had now the strife compos'd ;

He seiz'd the moment, and Quadrille propos'd ;

In hopes, when fairly once engag'd in play,

They could not leisure find so much to say.—    225

But soon the youth these hopes abortive found ;

Ten cards to each were scarcely dealt around,

When one, to *pass* by poverty constrain'd,

Against her luck in accents loud complain'd.

The next, who oft enquir'd, with anxious care,    230

Of red and black how many trumps there were,

Remain'd awhile on doubt's uncertain ground,

And sought advice from all the table round :

If *leave* she *ask'd*, the game was too secure ;

Nor would her cards permit her to *obscure*.    235

Resolv'd at last to win or hazard all,

She boldly ventur'd for a *king to call*.

But

But now the third, who long had filent fate,
And heard with wicked joy the deep debate,
At once *fanfprendre*'s pow'r refiftlefs claim'd,        240
And with exalted voice her trumps proclaim'd.
Thus fairly ftarted ev'ry nimble tongue,
And all the houfe with terms of fcience rung;
While now the *vole* was loft, and now *codille*,
And *hearts*, and *matadores*, and *forc'd fpadille*.*        245

---

\* The author having here adopted the French mode of
playing quadrille, as admitting of the greateft variety of defcription, it will be proper to explain fome of the terms, which
may not be familiar to the Englifh reader.

*Obfcuring* (v. 235) is that mode of playing in partnerfhip,
by which, when you have three good fuits in your hand, you
leave the choice of trumps from amongft them to the perfon
who happens to hold the king of the fourth.

*Calling*, or rather *taking a king*, (v. 237) is a cautious method of playing alone, by the affiftance of a king of any fuit
but trumps, borrowed, or rather bought from another hand.
                        See ACADEMIE DES JEUX.

# W H I S T.

## CANTO III.

C

# ARGUMENT.

Continuation of the ftory of Moody and his Aunts,
including the invention of the game of Whift.

Not any boaſt of ſkill, but extreme ſhift.

MILTON.

Quis potis eſt dignum pollenti pectore carmen
Condere, pro rerum majeſtate, hiſque repertis ?
Quiſve valet verbis tantum, qui fundere laudes
Pro meritis ejus poſſit, qui talia nobis
Pectore parta ſuo, quæſitaque præmia liquit ?

LUCRETIUS.

FOR three long winter months in chat or play
The ſocial ev'nings thus had paſs'd away ;
Till, once of life and all its comforts tir'd,
The youth indignant to his couch retir'd :
There to his ſick'ning ſoul whilſt all below          5
Seem'd but a weary length of hopeleſs woe,
* In this black channel did his muſings flow.

    " How have I this deſerv'd, ye pow'rs divine ?
" † For what offence, what grievous ſin of mine,

* In this black channel would my ravings run.
YOUNG's NIGHT THOUGHTS, vii. 652.

† Oh, what is my ſin ? what is my ſin ?
B. JONSON's SILENT WOMAN, Act 2, Sc. 2.

C 2

" An

" Am I condemn'd in this terreſtrial hell,        10

" This den of ſtrife, this windmill dome* to dwell ?

" Nor wealth nor fame have e'er engrofs'd my care;

" For peace alone I breath'd my fervent pray'r :

" And yet ſtern fate the humble ſuit denies,

" And ſtill beyond my reach the bleſſing flies.        15

" Thrice happy fire, within thy dark retreat,

" Of ſacred reſt the bleſt eternal ſeat ;

" Where no rude found invades thy ſilence deep,

" Alarms thine ear, or breaks thy quiet ſleep :

" While here thy wretched ſon muſt waſte his

        life        20

" In the dire whirlpool of perpetual ſtrife ;

" And fees, alas ! no profpect of repofe,

" Till death at laſt his weary eyes ſhall cloſe."

While thus he lay, reſign'd to grief's controul,

A ray of ſudden light illum'd his ſoul ;        25

* I dwell in a windmill.

B. JONSON's SILENT WOMAN, Act 5, Sc. 3.

Invention's

nvention's godlike pow'r his breaſt inſpir'd,

And eager hope his bright'ning ſpirit fir'd.

" Had I the happy ſkill ſome game to find,

" Whoſe charms ſo ſtrongly might attach the mind,

" And for ſuch ſtrict, ſevere attention call,  30

" As could not fail to ſtop the tongues of all.

" Suppoſe impartial chance two pairs to bind,

" In leagues offenſive and defenſive join'd ;

" Nor ſide by ſide allow the friends to ſit,

" But each in front of each at diſtance ſit :  35

" There while each card retain'd its native place,

" Unleſs the lord of all, th' imperial ace,

" None ſhould, as in Quadrille, be uſeleſs found,

" But, one by one, the pack be dealt around ;

" Thirteen to each, until the laſt of all,  40

" Which turning up, the dealer Trump ſhould call.

" But when the ſtrife begins, on either ſide,

" Tricks to ſecure let ev'ry art be tried ;

" For each new *lift*, when ſix are gain'd before,

" Shall with another point augment the Score.  45

  " Nor

" Nor yet alone fhould fkill the fcore advance,

" For fomewhat always muft be left to chance.

" Before another *deal*, let each demand

" How many *honours* grac'd his partner's hand ;

" And joining ftocks, proceed to reckon thofe    50

" By which their number overtop'd their foes :

" By two and two fhould fate the band divide,

" Their prefence then fhall better neither fide ;

" But three, where'er they fall, for two fhall
       count,

" And four fhall reckon for the whole amount.    55

" On fuch conditions let the ftrife proceed,

" And *deal* to *deal*, and *trump* to *trump* fucceed,

" Till thofe of better luck, or better play,

" Shall reckon ten, and bear the palm away.

" And at the goal fhould either fide arrive     60

" Before the others reach the point of five,

" The conqu'ring pair may then with juftice claim

" The praife and profit of a double game.

                     " But

" But one defeat fhould ne'er the conteft clofe,

" Nor yet the victors from their toils repofe,   65

" Till they have firft a fecond game obtain'd,

" And count a couple for the *rubber* gain'd."

When Archimedes at his bathing hour,

Infpir'd at laft by fome propitious pow'r,

The knotty problem folv'd, with which in vain   70

He long had rack'd his geometric brain;

It ftands recorded, that the raptur'd fage*,

To whom each little moment feem'd an age,

---

* Archimeden de bia tôn diagrammatôn apofpôntes funélei-
phon hoi therapontes. Ho de epi tés koilias egraphe ta fchemata
té ftlengidi, kai louomenos, hôs phafin, ek tés huperchufeôs en-
noéfas, tén tou ftephanou metréfin, hoion ek tinos katochés é
epipnoías, exélato boôn, Hewraika.

PLUTARCH, fed ubi haud fcio.

Tunc is (Archimedes) cum haberet ejus rei curam, cafu
venit in Balneum, ibique cum in folium defcenderet, animad-
vertit quantum corporis fui in eo infideret, tantum aquæ extra
folium effluere. Itaque cum ejus rei rationem explicationis of-
fendiffet, non eft moratus, fed exiluit gaudio motus de folio, et
nudus vadens domum verfus, fignificabat, clarâ voce, inveniffe
quod quæreret. Nam currens identidem Græcè clamabat,
Hewraika, Hewraika.

VITRUVIUS, lib. ix. cap. 3.

Till all the town his mental triumph knew,

While from the bath with eager hafte he flew,          75

Forgot he was not all compos'd of mind,

And left his breeches and his fhirt behind.

As thro' the ftreets he then *hewraika** cried,

With all the ftrength of fcientific pride,          ,

The boys and girls, attracted by the found,          80

From ev'ry lane and alley flock'd around ;

With wond'ring eyes his naked wifdom view'd,

And with triumphant fhouts his flight purfu'd.

Our hero thus forgot the darken'd room,

Sprung from his couch, and ftalk'd acrofs the gloom :

But tho' perhaps with equal rapture feiz'd,          86

And ftill more juftly with his triumph pleas'd,

Could yet in decent bounds his joy reftrain,

And very wifely went to bed again.

* A Greek word, which fignifies, *I have it.* This is by no
means the firft time in which it has appeared in Englifh poetry —

" Cries, Eῦρηκα ; the mighty fecret's found.''
                    DRYDEN's RELIGIO LAICI, 43.

One ſleepleſs night had paſs'd entire away, 90
And more than half of the ſucceeding day,
Before the youth, by dint of patient thought,
His noble ſcheme to full perfection brought.
But when amuſement's hour arriv'd again,
And cards, as uſual, took their turn to reign, 95
He kept no longer to himſelf confin'd
The bright conception of his plaſtic mind:
But (while exulting hope and conſcious pride
Unwonted boldneſs to his ſpeech ſupplied)
Declar'd, that if the venerable three 100
Would deign his pupils for a time to be,
He could a game unfold entirely new,
Yet practis'd only by a choſen few;
And which he truſted would amuſe them more
Than any other they had play'd before. 105

A point like this our hero gain'd with eaſe;
For novelty is ſure the ſex to pleaſe.
With ſoft addreſs, and faſcinating art,
Behold him next perform the tutor's part.

Hard

Hard was the task, ideas to explain,                    110
Which yet but vaguely floated thro' his brain;
And paint the changing hues of shadowy thought,
Not yet by practice to confiftence brought.—
But this he did as far as words could do:
A gentle hint was flily added too,                      115
On ftrict attention, and referve of tongue,
How greatly here the hopes of triumph hung.

    Now Chance, invok'd, a mate affign'd to each,
And three fat down to learn, and one to teach.
The nimble cards around the table ran;                  120
The trump look'd upward, and the ftrife began.
In that propitious hour the world's delight,
The game of filence, firft beheld the light;
Not the rude light of nature's glaring ray,
But art's politer, more congenial day;                  125
From tapers planted thick the table round,
Or pendent lamps, with flaming radiance crown'd.
Each future age fhall blefs that golden hour,
And hail with rapture its extenfive pow'r,

                              Which

Which came, our life with luftre to adorn,          13●
Big with the fate of gamefters yet unborn.

The fifterhood at firft forgot the change,
And ftill, as ufual, left their tongues to range;
For pow'rful habit is not foon fuppreft,
And female tongues were never form'd for reft.  135
But when they found, feverely to their coft,
That they were fure to lofe who fpoke the moft,
That potent voice, which feldom pleads in vain,
Regard to int'reft, and the love of gain,
By flow degrees fuppreft each idle found,          14●
And ev'ry lip with chains of filence bound.
Some torrent thus from wint'ry mountains long
With foam and fury pours its waves along,
And rolling onward with impetuous found,
O'erflows its banks, and deafens all around :       145
But when the fummer comes, and with him brings
The thirfty fpirit on his glowing wings,
By flow degrees the liquid ftores decay,
And the rough roar in murmurs dies away;
Until, at laft, its voice is heard no more,          15●
And filence reigns where all was noife before.

# W H I S T.

## CANTO IV.

## ARGUMENT.

Sequel of the ſtory of Moody and his **Aunts**; including
the laws of the game of Whiſt.

Laws, wife as nature, and as fixt as fate.

Pope.

BUT tho' confusion's voice was heard no more,
And silence reign'd where all was noise before;
Yet still at times occasions would arise,
Where all restraint the sisters could despise;
And still disturb the youth's unlucky state          5
With all the violence of keen debate.—
Perhaps the dealer might the cards confuse,
Nor yet her privilege could bear to lose:
Perhaps a card might on the table fall—
Its mistress never meant to play at all;             10
Who then her error might lament in vain,
And urge her right to take it up again:
Perhaps her haste a trick with trumps had gain'd,
While of the suit her hand a card retain'd—

A fa

A fad miftake; which, when it once was found,    15
In endlefs ftrife embroil'd the table round :
Or, worfe than all, perhaps oblivion's pow'r
Had mifs'd entirely *fcoring*'s proper hour ;
And now too late thofe honours rofe to mind,
Which to their tricks they might have juftly join'd; 20
A lofs which never pafs'd from mem'ry's fight,
But clouded ftill each after triumph bright,
And fill'd with murmur's voice  the whole repin-
      ing night.

   All this young Moody with difpleafure faw,
And vainly ftrove to keep the ftorm in awe :      25
From this he found, that, tho' fo much was done,
He had not wholly yet the battle won ;
From this he knew, that fomewhat ftill remain'd,
Ere filence here a perfect triumph gain'd.
Oft had he read that tracks of fertile ground,     30
With lavifh nature's richeft bounty crown'd,
In rude neglect and favage wildnefs lay,
To defolation and to wafte a prey ;

                                             For

For this one single but important cause,

The want of regular and wholesome laws. 35

And, since capricious fortune's blind controul

Had thus already made his favour'd soul

The bold discov'rer of a region new,

Resolv'd to prove its legiflator too.

    Nor did the strength of his inventive mind 40

This second task an arduous duty find :

For two short hours of one tempestuous day

Suffic'd to range his laws in neat array ;

And, lest his subjects might, perhaps, disdain

The recent offspring of his youthful brain, 45

His prudent art a cautious method chose,

And feign'd (for fiction well each lawyer knows)

That he these laws had in the pages found

Of one whose genius had been long renown'd.

Succefs, as usual, crown'd his artful plan, 50

And, leave of reading gain'd, he thus began.

I. The

### I.

The cards to fhuffle long as may him fuit,
Is ev'ry player's right, without difpute :
But when this right thro' all the hands has pafs'd,
Still with the dealer it fhould reft at laft ;      55
Who, ere he deals, fhould have the painted band
Cut by the perfon on his better hand ;
As elfe th' unlawful deal will never ftand.

### II.

If in the pack a card difplay its face,
\* He muft begin again in fuch a cafe :      60
And fhould he one in dealing chance to turn,
The foes, if fo inclin'd, that deal may fpurn.

### III.

But if he gives not each his number due,
To one too many, or to one too few,

\* Vide Hoyle, chap. xviii. laws xi. and ix.

He

\* He then muſt be content the deal to loſe,    65
Unleſs his luck ſupplies the ſole excuſe,
That, while he dealt, by either of the foes
The cards were touch'd; for then we may ſuppoſe
From them, and not from him, the fault aroſe.

## IV.

Still on the board, the whole commencing round,
† Let his trump card expos'd to view be found : 71
Nor, after that, tho' you may trumps enquire,
Can you of it another ſight deſire.

## V.

Let each, before he play, his hand review,
And mark if he poſſeſs the number due ;    75
‡ For ſhould he not, and yet proceed to play,
Till he perceives at laſt a card away,
He muſt for each *revoke* the forfeit pay.

---

\* Vide Hoyle, chap. xxii. law xiii.

† Id. chap. xviii. law xviii.

‡ Id. ibid. law xii.

VI. Let

### VI.

Let each with conftant eye the board furvey,
* Nor afk another what he chanc'd to play,      80
Tho' he may bid him draw his card away.

### VII.

Nor here, as in your former game, Quadrille,
May one examine all the tricks at will :
The lateft can alone return to fight ;
The reft muft ne'er again behold the light.      85

### VIII.

The card which once has fairly touch'd the board,
Muft never more be to the hand reftor'd.

### IX.

When, from miftake, as it at times proceeds,
The one rafh partner for the other leads ;
† Then may the foes a juft occafion feize,      90
To make his brother play what fuit they pleafe ;

<hr>

" Hoyle, chap. xxii. law viii.
† Id. chap. xviii. law i.

                                         And

And for that card, which was fo keen to fall,
They have a right at any time to call.

## X.

For each *revoke* your foe may chance to make,
From his collected tricks you three can take;          95
Or from his fcore  (if tricks he yet has none)
* Take down three points, or add them to your own :
But  this to do you ne'er can urge the right,
Until the trick is turn'd, and out of fight ;
Tho' then its influence boafts a fairer claim          100
Than any other fcore in all the game.

## XI.

The tricks, fair children of fuperior fkill,
Before the cafual honours reckon ftill.

## XII.

Remember always, when the hand is o'er,
† At once your honours and your tricks to fcore ;   105

* Hoyle, chap. xviii. laws iii. and ii.
† Id. ibid. law vi.

For fhould you wait till trumps be turn'd again,
Your right you then may claim, but claim in vain.

## XIII.

But if beyond the truth you chance to go,
Your fcore diminifh'd muft enrich the foe.

## XIV.

The proper feafon on your friend to *call*,          110
\* Is juft before your hand a card lets fall;
A moment later, and you lofe the claim,
And ev'n a moment fooner is the fame.

## XV.

† But when the trump has once appear'd in fight,
Let none remind his friend of calling's right.          115

## XVI.

Altho' of tricks one fide fhould make them all,
That rareft triumph which a *flam* we call,

\* Hoyle, chap. xviii. law xxii.
† Id. ibid. law v.

Yet

Yet they from this no profit e'er muſt claim,
Which would not ſuit the ſpirit of the game.

---

Such were the Laws, which now to all appear    120
So juſt, ſo uſeful, ſo conciſe, and clear,
That one conſenting voice, without delay,
Engag'd their future influence to obey :
And ſhould he doubt their word, for ſanction's
      ſake,
They proffer'd too, that very hour, to take    125
Whatever oath he might be pleas'd to make.

The youth delighted made a penſive pauſe,
And riſing to their ſight diſplay'd the laws :
Then the three ſiſters held their hands on high,
While each upon the ceiling fixt her eye ;     130
And, all in decent order thus diſpos'd,
He then in ſolemn tone his oath propos'd.

" By Tea and Scandal's ever dear delights ;
" By Liberty of ſpeech, that firſt of rights ;

     " That

" That right which virgins, wives, and widows
          claim,                              135
" To use all freedom with their neighbour's fame;
" By all the Joys that pensive mem'ry knows,
" When to that glorious time she backward goes,
" When o'er your days the pow'r of courtship
          threw
" The magic lustre of his brilliant hue;      140
" Whose musky breath perfum'd each precious
          hour
" With the sweet scent of pleasure's myrtle bow'r:
" By those Regrets which now your bosoms feel,
" That virgin pride had arm'd your hearts with
          steel,
" And made you deaf to ev'ry lover's pray'r,   145 ⎫
" Till they at last resign'd the fruitless care,      ⎬
" And left you to repentance and despair:          ⎭
" And by those Hopes which yet your fancies fill, ⎫
" That, aided by your own alluring skill,            ⎬
" Propitious fortune will permit you still      150 ⎭
                    7
                              " With

" With feſtive pomp to deck the bridal day,

" And paſs the night in nuptial joys away."

Such was that Oath, of ſtrength unknown before;

By whoſe emphatic words the ſiſters ſwore :

Nor need I ſurely add, that they tranſgreſs'd no

      more.                      155

# W H I S T.

## CANTO V.

# ARGUMENT.

Whift long of coming into repute.—Comparative eftimate of its beauties.—Firft excellence, its promotion of filence.—Digreffive excurfion to the play-houfe; and fcheme for the improvement of theatrical entertain. ments,

Ma, d'un parlar ne l'altro, ove fon ite
Si lungi dal cammin ch'io facev' ora ?
Non lo credo però fi aver fmarrito,
Ch'io non lo fappia ritrovare ancora.

ARIOSTO.

HOW flow, at firft, is ftill the growth of fame,
And what obftructions wait each rifing name !
The brighteft efforts of invention's brain
Can ne'er at once extenfive notice gain.
Our ftupid fathers thus neglected long                5
The glorious boaft of Milton's epic fong ;
While Waller's weak, and Cowley's rugged line
Were read with rapture, and pronounc'd divine.
And thus, when this our century was young,
(If we may truft what comic bards have fung*)         10

Vide Congreve, Vanbrugh, Cibber, Farquhar, Centlivre, &c.
paffim.

Whilft

\* Whilſt Ombre and Quadrille at court were us'd,

† And Baſſet's pow'r the city dames amus'd,

Imperial Whiſt was yet but light eſteem'd,

And paſtime fit for none but ruſtics deem'd.

‡ When Sullen's wife bewails her wretched ſtate, 15

Condemn'd for life to ſuch a ſurly mate,

---

\* Ombre (ſays Sir Francis Wronghead) is a geam at cards, that the better ſort of people play three together at.

PROVOKED HUSBAND, Act 2, Sc. 7.

To ſpoil the nation's laſt great trade, Quadrille.

POPE's MORAL ESSAYS, iii. 76.

† Vide Centlivre's Baſſet-Table, and Vanbrugh's City Wives' Confederacy.

‡ DORINDA. You ſhare in all the pleaſures that the country affords.

MRS. SULLEN. Country pleaſures! racks and torments! Doſt think, child, that my limbs are made for leaping of ditches, and clambering over ſtyles? or that my parents, wiſely foreſeeing my future happineſs in country pleaſures, had early inſtructed me in the rural accompliſhments of drinking fat ale, playing at Whiſk, and ſmoaking tobacco with my huſband.

FARQUHAR's BEAUX STRATAGEM, Act 2, Sc. 1.

She

She hints, that, had her parents wifer been,

And all the rigour of her fate forefeen,

They fhould have taught her, with an early care,

In all the country's vulgar joys to fhare ;            20

Acrofs a five-barr'd gate her neck to rifque,

To drink fat ale, to fmoak, and play at *Whifk*.

But Milton's mufe at laft a critic* found,

Who fpread his praife o'er all the world around ;

And Hoyle at length for Whift perform'd the fame,

And prov'd its right to univerfal fame.            26

What game indeed, of all the num'rous lift,

In point of beauty, can compare to Whift ?

Or which, of all where gold was ever loft,

So rich a catalogue of charms can boaft ?            30

And firft, how great its pow'r, in chains of gold,

Without conftraint, the willing tongue to hold !

That nimble, wicked, wild, rebellious thing,

Which reafon feldom can to order bring,

* Vide Addifon's Critique on the Paradife Loft.

When

When ladies fair convene, their tea to fip,       35
And fcandal's fpirit fits on ev'ry lip,
Impatient fits, until its turn arrive,
Then burfts like bees impetuous from their hive,
(Alas! that words which bear a mortal fting
* From fuch a charming honied houfe fhould fpring!)
How fatal then the vile malicious rage,       41
Which fpares nor rank nor merit, fex nor age;
That rage, whofe direful havock to reftrain,
Virtue is weak, and friendfhip pleads in vain!
But now let Whift appear, in regal tone,       45
Commanding filence from his verdant throne;
And, lo! at once the vocal ftorm fubfides;
Each accent now in gentle whifpers glides;
The harfh difcordant notes of rancour ceafe,
And all is love, and unity, and peace.       50
  When frefh from college, in the crowded pit,
I us'd at firft with panting heart to fit;

* Javabi telkhi mizcibed lebi lali fhekerkhara'
                              HAFEZ.

                                   Whilft

Whilſt all the charms theatric pleaſures boaſt
Had not as yet their virgin graces loſt;
And ev'ry word I from the ſtage could hear 55
Was boundleſs rapture to my youthful ear;
How often have I curs'd the buzzing ſound,
Which flow'd continual from the boxes round!
And wiſh'd our fine folks would adopt the mode,
Which travellers report prevails abroad*; 60

Where

---

* The Opera at Florence is a place where the people of qua-
lity pay and receive viſits, and converſe as freely as at the Caſino
above-mentioned. This occaſions a continual paſſing and re-
paſſing to and from the boxes, except in thoſe where there is a
party of cards formed; it is then looked on as a piece of ill
manners to diſturb the players. I never was more ſurpriſed,
than when it was propoſed to me to make one of a whiſt party,
in a box which ſeemed to have been made for the purpoſe, with
a little table in the middle. I hinted that it would be full as con-
venient to have the party ſomewhere elſe: but I was told, good
muſic added greatly to the pleaſure of a whiſt party; that it in-
creaſed the joy of good fortune, and ſoothed the affliction of bad.
As I thought the people of this country better acquainted than
myſelf with the power of muſic, I conteſted the point no longer;

but

Where Whift thro' all the night in filence reigns,

And ev'ry box a gaming fet contains ;

Who, while more ferious fcenes their thoughts engage,

Have feldom leifure to regard the ftage.

But now (for time increafe of wifdom brings) 65

How widely diff'rent is my fenfe of things !

Since knowledge of the world enlarg'd my mind,

And knowledge of the town my tafte refin'd :

Yet ftill I curfe—but not the charming found

Which flows continual from the boxes round ;       70

I curfe thofe rants of wild unmeaning rage,

Which rife inceffant from the noify ftage ;

Which o'er the found of modifh tongues prevail,

Deprive me oft of many a curious tale,

And drown the fmooth addrefs of many a peer,     75

Before its meaning reach my anxious ear.

but have generally played two or three rubbers at whift in the
ftage-box every opera night.

Dr. Moore, Lett. lxxiii.

Here

Here let me paufe, a project to explain,
Which more than once has ftruck my fertile brain ;
And which to publifh, my impatient mind
May ne'er perhaps a fitter feafon find.          80

  That dome, whofe managers inceffant ftrive
To keep the public appetite alive,
 And feed their guefts, on each returning night,
With varied treats of ever new delight ;
Where yet delight is often fought in vain,          85
And languor and difguft too often reign ;
One fimple change might to a temple turn,
Where pleafure's lamp could never fail to burn.
How rich a feaft would ev'ry play become,
If, like a pantomime, the fcenes were dumb ;          90
And liberty of fpeech to none allow'd,
But thofe diftinguifh'd from the vulgar crowd ;
Who, thron'd betwixt the galleries and pit,
In vaulted cabinets of fplendor fit !
We fhould not then frequent the houfe to know  95
What Hamlet faid a thoufand years ago :

But

But flock to catch, in the politeſt way,
The news and ſcandal of the preſent day.
What perfect bliſs from ſuch a ſcheme appears
* To all our faculties of eyes and ears !          100
The one delighted with the charms that flow
From graceful action, and the pomp of ſhow;
The other raviſh'd with the full diſplay
Of all that wit and elegance could ſay.

A plan which promis'd thus their toils to eaſe, 105
The ſlothful players could not fail to pleaſe ;
Nor would it coſt them one triumphant hour,
Or circumſcribe their faſcinating pow'r.

For ſure the SIDDONS, whoſe expreſſive eye
Each pauſe of language can ſo well ſupply,          110
Requires no ſuccour from poetic art
To rouſe, to ſoften, or to tear the heart ;
Which, were it made of penetrable ſtuff,
Would find her geſtures and her looks enough.

* The very faculty of eyes and ears.
                    SHAKSPEAR'S HAMLET, Act 2, Sc. 8.

                                        Nor

Nor lefs applaufe would crown the graces wild  115
Of fportive JORDAN, Nature's charming child ;
Whofe romps*, tho' mute, would be refiftlefs ftill,
† And all the houfe with endlefs laughter fill.

But much as thofe would love the change who fit
Or in the boxes, or the crowded pit ;                120
I fear thofe vulgar fouls, who perch'd on high
Behold improvement with a jealous eye,
Would loudly all againft the motion cry.
But managers would from their duty ftray,
Did they to fuch a voice attention pay ;             125
Or rifque offending the politer few,
To pleafe the tafte of fuch a taftelefs crew.
Befides at times, or even once a week,
A play for them might be allow'd to fpeak.

* Vide Prifcilla Tomboy, Mifs Hoyden, Mifs Prue, Peggy,
the Virgin Unmafk'd, &c.

† Afbeftos d'ar enôrto Gelôs, makareffi Theoifin.
HOMER's ILIAD, i. 599.

\* The Orphan then, or some such vulgar thing, 130
Might 'prentice girls and country boobies bring ;
† Who there might all in maudlin concert whine,
And wet their handkerchiefs at ev'ry line ;

> \* The tender poet of domestic woe,
> Whose Orphan, wedded in a luckless hour,
> Oft as her story on the scene appears,
> In all the native eloquence of grief,
> Spite of that monster Fashion's impious rage,
> Calls from the gen'ral eye a vulgar tear.

This unfashionable rant is taken from a late poem, entitled, The
Choice (c. iii. 114) ; which is full of affectation, bombast, and
romanticity ; which abounds with antediluvian notions about love
and friendship, virtue and taste ; and in which there is not the
smallest knowledge of the world, nor the least attempt at wit or humour.  But what makes the passage above quoted still more ridi-
culous than it would otherwise have been, is its being put into the
mouth of Avarice ; a personage, who, though none of the votaries
of fashion, was never remarkable, so far as I have heard, for being
fond of dropping the tears of sensibility : a striking proof into
what gross blunders those authors are apt to fall, who give them-
selves up to the guidance of enthusiasm, and allow their fancy to
run away with their judgment.

> † No crowds may be let in, no maudlin gazers,
> To wet their handkerchiefs, and make report,
> How like a saint she ended.
>                    ROWE's L. JANE GRAY, Act 5, Sc. 1.

And

And (filly fouls !) to fhew their forrow, ftrive
That fhe fhould die who never was alive :     135
While we devoted the remaining nights
To thofe refin'd and elegant delights,
Which none can relifh but the chofen band,
The flow'r and cream of each admiring land ;
Who down the fmooth expanfe of fafhion's tide
In pleafure's painted barge fecurely glide,     141
And o'er the glitt'ring wave in fplendid triumph
      ride.

Perhaps the furly critic here will fay,
That I have grofsly wander'd from my way ;
And afk me what connection can fubfift     145
Betwixt my project and the game of Whift ?
But moft of thofe who may the fong perufe,
That public fpirit will, I truft, excufe,
Which led me thus the rules of art to fpurn,
And leave my theme—to which I now return ;     150
But in another Canto, if you pleafe,
Both for my own, and for the reader's eafe :

For this, tho' fhort, too much of fenfe contains,

Not to be kept apart from lighter ftrains;

And having from the point fo far digrefs'd,        155

\* My wearied mufe requires a little reft.

---

\* Non più, Signor, non più di quefto canto,
    Ch'io fon già rauco, e vo' pofarmi alquanto.
                ARIOSTO, ORLANDO FURIOSO, xiv. 134.

# W H I S T.

## CANTO VI.

# ARGUMENT.

Comparative eſtimate of Whiſt reſumed.—Second excellence, its ſuperiority of intereſt.—Third, its inde-
pendence on the principle of avarice ; and, in conſe-
quence of this, its connection with economy.—Story
of Cardelia and Sir John Gormaw.

No hay que dudar, fino que efta arte y exercicio excede á todas aquellas
y aquellos que los hombres inventaron.

CERVANTES.

LET all the games that afk but little fkill,
Loo, Commerce, Comet, Baffet, and Quadrille,
Like twinkling ftars that dimly gild the night,
Shrink from the blaze of Whift's refulgent light :
Nay more, let thofe that higher rank may claim,     5
Let nice Piquette, and Ombre's ftudious game,
(Tho' each has charms) the fruitlefs conteft yield,
And to the filent fport refign the field.
For which of thefe can boaft the pow'r to bind
In chains of equal ftrength the captive mind ?     10
Can each, or all, fuch anxious thought infpire,
Or with fuch ardour keen the fpirit fire ?
Can they fo much the lofer's peace deftroy,
Or fill the winner's breaft with equal joy ?

Can

Can, at Piquette, the *huitieme* and *quatorze*;        15

Quadrille's triumvirate of *matadores*;

*Fifteens* at Cribbidge, or the *pam* at Loo;

With such ecstatic rapture bless the view,

As when at Whist the firm quadruple band

Of honour'd chiefs enrich a single hand ?        20

Or, what is oft of more importance found,

When strength of *cards* with strength of *trumps* is

          crown'd ?

  But some will here object, that such applause,

So far from helping, rather hurts the cause;

Since all will grant that pastimes were design'd,   25

* Not to employ, but to relieve the mind;

And therefore those that leave it most at ease

Have surely far the fairest claim to please.

But they that argue thus from sense depart,

And know but little of the human heart;        30

---

\* Cards were at first for benefits design'd;
          Sent to amuse, and not enslave the mind.
                EPILOGUE TO THE GAMESTER, 30.

                                        Which

Which not in pleafure's felf can pleafure find,
Unlefs it comes with agitation join'd ;
Which bafking warm in fortune's funfhine clear,
Sighs for the fhifting clouds of hope and fear ;
And tir'd with looking on the liftlefs deep,                35
When lull'd by fummer gales to filver fleep,
Would rather far the tempeft's fury brave,
When danger rides on ev'ry foaming wave.

Let Ombre then amufe the fons of Spain,
And ftill Piquette the Frenchman's game remain ;
Let Brag be left to Newgate's brazen crew,                41
To children Commerce, and to footmen Loo ;
While ev'ry Briton, who to manly fenfe,
To tafte, or breeding has the leaft pretence,
His fportive hours to Whift alone confines,                45
And other paftimes all for this refigns.

How oft with indignation have I feen
The tables fet two taftelefs fools between ;
Who, tho' in all the rational delight
Of peaceful Whift they could have pafs'd the night ; 50

Yet

Yet (ftrange to tell !) preferr'd Backgammon's noife,

Its artlefs efforts, and its flender joys ;

And fate them down, their ftupid fkill to try,

* Regardlefs of the pair that waited by,

Left to the fport of betting who fhould win,          55

And lift'ning to the dice's rattling din ;

Or, fhould that paftime not amufe them long,

To yawn, to barter fnuff, or hum a fong.

---

* A fimilar picture of negligent impolitenefs, and a fimilar inftance of depravity of tafte (fubftituting only Piquette for Backgammon), occurs at the end of the firft chapter of Mrs. Smith's new novel, the Reclufe of the Lake : " Mifs Newenden and Davenant then fat down to Piquette ; and Sir Edward and Ethelinde were left to entertain each other with a book, or fuch converfation as the occurrences or remarks of the day afforded them."

But I would not advife any future Bifhop, who may think proper to write upon the Marks of Imitation, to produce as an example this acknowledged refemblance ; as the author of this poem is ready to make oath, before any *critical* court in Chriftendom, that the lines upon Backgammon are entirely original ; and that it was nearly four months after they were written, before he knew that Ethelinde had a being.

Long has the mufe effay'd her voice to raife,

And reach the height of Whift's tranfcendent praife;

And yet the fubject muft not be refign'd, 61

While much its proudeft boaft remains behind—

A boaft furpaffing far each rival dow'r,

The boaft of pleafure's independent pow'r;

Whilft all the games that for precedence ftrive 65

From avarice alone their charms derive.

For who is he, without an ample ftake,

To play Piquette could e'er the trouble take,

Tho' fure, each other *deal, repique* to find,

Or with a humbler *pique, capot* conjoin'd? 70

And at Quadrille, how carelefs and how cool,

Without the profpect of a tempting *pool*,

Would ev'n the man remain, whofe brilliant hand

Could ftill *fanfprendre*, or the *vole* command!

But he whom Whift's bewitching fpirit fires, 75

From mercenary hopes no aid requires;

But fits with patience, night fucceeding night,

And deals the cards with ever new delight;

(Tho'

(Tho' barren conqueſt no reward can claim,

And only differs from defeat in name) 80

Bleſt in the pow'r his victories to tell,

And in the conſcious pride of playing well.

Seems it not clear, from what has juſt been ſaid,

That all profeſſors of the rhyming trade,

Whoſe pockets now (whatever elſe they hold) 85

Are ſeldom loaded with a weight of gold,

And who for paſtime rarely much can pay,

At independent Whiſt ſhould learn to play ;

And grateful ſtill each fair occaſion ſeize,

To celebrate with zeal its pow'r to pleaſe ? 90

And yet that bard, whoſe ſweet deſcriptive tongue

With ſuch applauſe the varying ſeaſons ſung,

Has dar'd with Scottiſh rancour to defame,

\* And tax as dull, this animated game.

---

\* To cheat the thirſty moments, Whiſt awhile
Walks his dull round, beneath a cloud of ſmoke,
Wreath'd, fragrant from the pipe.
THOMSON's AUTUMN, 524.

This

This one rafh word has all his fame defac'd,        95
And robb'd his mufe of ey'ry claim to tafte.

   And thus can Whift, with pleafure's richeft dow'r,
Conjoin the boaft of economic pow'r—
No fingle boaft ; but one whofe fkilful ufe,
At times, in various ways, can thrift produce.        100
And now let all who hold their money dear,
Lend to my frugal tale a ferious ear.

   Cardelia at the age of forty-one
Was left a widow by her honeft man ;
Who long, in fondnefs, had indulg'd his dear  105
* In drums, and routs, and fuch expenfive gear,
Beyond the rate his income well could bear.
But when th' uxorious fool his life refign'd,
The cruel income would not ftay behind.
So faithful to the hufband all his life,        110
'Twas furely fhabby to defert the wife,

* But mice, and rats, and fuch fmall gear.
       SHAKESPEAR's LEAR, Act 3, Sc. 7.

F        At

At such a time, when all was dark around,

And hope or comfort nowhere to be found ;

And well it knew, the vile malicious thing,

That it alone could solid comfort bring.          115

Misfortunes here come always in a train :

Two such at once what mortal could sustain ?

" Alas !" she cried, in hopeless sorrow lost,

" Was ever woman thus by Fortune cross'd ?

" To wed a husband who could please his wife, 120

" And make her happy—only all his life !

" How blest is she, to whom her wealthy mate,

" Whenever summon'd by the call of fate,

" The pangs of separation to relieve,

" Some solid tokens of his love can leave !          125

" To her perhaps devolves, in full command,

" Some livelong property of jointure land ;

" Where thro' the gloom of many a shady grove

" The pensive mourner may securely rove ;

" And where her eye, when spent with wasting grief,

" From many a verdant lawn may find relief.          131

5

" But

" But my ambition would not foar fo high;

" Far lefs to me would happinefs fupply;

" Whofe fober wifhes afk from fate no more,

" Than juft to live as I have liv'd before; 135

" And ftill at times my focial band invite,

" To pafs in charming Whift the tedious night,

" And when the bus'nefs of the night was paft,

" Repay their prefence with a flight repaft.

" But hopes like thefe, tho' humble in their kind, 140

" Muft now, alas! for ever be refign'd;

" Since Fate's malignant pow'r my life purfues,

" And dooms the fad alternative to choofe—

" At home no more my fav'rite game to play,

" Or fend my party fupperlefs away." 145

 In deep defpondence funk, thus long fhe lay,

Till hope at laft reveal'd a glimpfe of day,

And touch'd her fancy with his golden ray:

Some friendly pow'r difpell'd the mift of fear,

And kindly whifper'd in her drooping ear 150

The

The falutary truth—that womankind,

By all the malice of their fates combin'd,

Of Fortune's gifts could ne'er be quite bereft,

While art or ingenuity was left.

'Twas now the queftion, how fhe fhould behave, 155

To keep her party, and her fupper fave.

In this refearch her waking hours were fpent,

And all her eager dreams on this were bent.

At laft fhe found it ; for a woman's brain,

That fought devices, never fought in vain.        160

    Tranfported now, her cards again fhe fends

To all the circle of her gaming friends ;

Where courtly words, arrang'd in order due,

Invited ftill to Whift, and fupper too.

They come, obedient to the welcome call,        165

And, compliments difpatch'd, to bus'nefs fall.

Succeffive *rubbers* lengthen'd out the night,

And ftill the fupper was not ready quite.

Till tir'd at laft with one accord they rife,

With aching heads, and fleep-defiring eyes.        170

                    And

And now th' aftonifh'd lady ftrives in vain
Her guefts a little longer to detain;
In vain regrets her good provifion loft,
And fomewhat mentions of a tedious roaft;
While each, politely hurrying down the ftairs,   175
A total want of appetite declares.

    Thus far fuccefs her vent'rous fcheme had crown'd,
And art's fair laurels wreath'd her temples round;
And yet fhe fear'd that, were fhe ftill to ufe
The fame contrivance, and the fame excufe,   180
They might at laft the fruitlefs call refufe.
But thofe whom cards with genuine paffion fire
Can ftill with eafe fupprefs each low defire;
And ev'n fubmit (to be indulg'd in play)
To faft, or, what were harder ftill, to pray:   185
And thus, regardlefs of her fober cheer,
True to the hour, Cardelia's guefts appear.
For many a night the felf-fame farce was play'd;
Some crofs event the banquet ftill delay'd;

         And

And ſtill the lazy cook, tho' warn'd before,          190
The blame of all, with little juſtice, bore;
Who would indeed have mighty wonders done,
Could ſhe have finiſh'd what was ne'er begun.
But all was manag'd with ſo much addreſs,
That none appear'd the humbling truth to gueſs;   195
Or, if they did, would not the fraud proclaim,
As ſupper was not that for which they came.

   Long might ſhe thus have ſhewn ſuperior ſenſe,
By keeping company without expence,
Had not a member of her gaming band          200
Yielded to give a baronet her hand;
And eager to diſplay her ſov'reign pow'r,
Brought her new huſband in an evil hour
For poor Cardelia.—Well the widow knew
Sir John Gormaw had come with groſſer view   205
Than did the reſt: and, tho' he thought that play
Did well enough to paſs the night away,
Was not the man to run ſo great a riſque,
As loſe a ſupper for a game at *Whiſk.*

                                But

But ftill fhe hop'd, whatever he might feel,        210
He would at leaft his difcontent conceal;
Nor fingly dare, in fuch a public way,
His vile difgraceful paffion to difplay;
Or, finding nothing could be got to eat,
He would at worft his vifit ne'er repeat.          215
    They came us ufual at the hour of feven,
And all went fmoothly on till near eleven;
When at the table where Cardelia fate,
Againft the bridal pair in keen debate,
The well-fought *rubber* happen'd to be done,      220
And ftraight another was of courfe begun—
A ftep not greatly to Sir John's content,
Whofe mind was now on other objects bent;
Who thought, whate'er the friends of Whift might
      fay,
That knife and fork was much fuperior play;        225
And would at fuch an hour have rather feen
One board in white, than fix array'd in green:

And yet, tho' such ideas fill'd his mind,
He still could keep them to himself confin'd.
But when at last he saw the *rubber* o'er,                    230
And matters standing as they stood before,
He thought it could not be a mighty crime,
Were he to hint that it was supper time.
To this was straight a ready answer made,
That one more *rubber* might with ease be play'd: 235
And poor Gormaw, tho' sore against his will,
Was forc'd, instead of rising, to sit still.
But that he did it with an aukward grace,
Appear'd too plainly from his troubled face;
Where discontent in ev'ry feature frown'd,             240
And hungry fury lour'd on all around.
-But time on ev'ry grief an end bestows,
And brought at length this *rubber* to a close;
And then indeed he deem'd relief was near,
And vow'd in secret that the lady's cheer             245
Thro' each successive dish should richly p
For such absurd, such barbarous delay.

                                        Yet

Yet vain the hope ; for, to his fad furprife,

The thoughtlefs widow ftill forgot to rife.

But when fhe took the cards again to deal,          256

The knight no longer could his foul conceal :

The fierce impatience of his craving maw

Forgot politenefs, decency, and awe ;

And, ftarting from his feat, he roundly fwore

He could not fupper want one moment more ;          255

Refolv'd that inftant to defcend, and know

What curfed reafon made the cook fo flow ;

And rather than the thing fhould longer ftand,

That he himfelf would lend a helping hand.

Cardelia then, with vifage pale as death,          260

While gafping terror almoft ftopt her breath :

" Dear fir—you muft not, cannot think to go ;—

" Be feated, fir—the maid will let us know."

Nor did his lady fail her aid to join,

And caught his fleeve to ftop his ftrange defign : 265

" Oh fie ! Sir John ; could you fo vulgar be ?

" Demean your dignity to that degree ?"

But

But all unmov'd Sir John their efforts bore,

Broke from them both, and hurried to the door.

As down the steps with eager haste he goes,        270

No fav'ry scent regales his gaping nose;

No merry jack, still whirling round and round,

Salutes his ear with banquet-boding sound.

But when at last the kitchen door he gains,

Surprise and horror thrill his shiv'ring veins :        275

Nought there one sign of preparation gave,

But all was dark, and quiet as the grave ;

Save what the glimm'ring moon reveal'd to view,

Which thro' the panes a faintish lustre threw,

And shew'd the drowsy, long-expecting maid,        280

Half naked, nodding by the fire decay'd ;

Where scatter'd embers feelingly declare

That one poor egg could scarce be roasted there.

As when some youth of firm and constant mind,

Who long in climes remote had absent pin'd ;        285

And, after many a year of toil and care,

Returns impatient to review the fair,

Whom

Whom ftill he fondly hopes to find the fame
Frefh blooming object of his youthful flame;
But fees, alas! that time's relentlefs pow'r      290
Has chang'd the bloffom to a faded flow'r;
For radiant locks, that wav'd in ringlets gay,
Sees rugged treffes verging faft to gray;
For eyes, whofe glance illumin'd all around,
Dull lifelefs lamps, in wat'ry dimnefs drown'd;   295
For cheeks, which glow'd with beauty's rofy pride,
A wan complexion, and a fhrivell'd hide—
One tender word he fcarce has pow'r to fay,
But turns with horror from the fight away.
His back Gormaw with equal horror turn'd;   300
With equal grief his difappointment mourn'd,
And mutt'ring curfes to the room return'd.

    Cardelia there had funk into a chair,
In fpeechlefs agony, and blank defpair;
On whom, the moment that fhe ftruck his view, 305
A ftern, indignant, furious glance he threw;

                              Nor

Nor deign'd to fpeak, but with **his angry eyes,**

While thus impatient to his wife he **cries:**

" Come, come, my lady, **let us hafte away,**

' Nor longer in this houfe of **famine ftay;**    310

" In fome cold vault, with duft and darknefs lin'd,

" We might as well a fupper hope to find.

" 'Tis all a curfed, vile, infernal plan;

" But henceforth let her cheat us if fhe can."

   **Thus all came out;** and with a gen'ral fneer   315

They **thank'd their hoftefs for** her princely cheer;

Then hurried off, and left the dame behind,

Not in the moft contented frame of mind.

She curs'd Gormaw; fhe fainted, rag'd, **aud cried;**

Nay, fome will go fo far to fay fhe died   320

(It hurt her vanity to that degree):

And if fhe did — why fo fhe might for me.

# WHIST.

## CANTO VII.

## ARGUMENT.

Apparent facility, and real difficulty of Whiſt.—Memory, Judgment, and Temper the three principal requiſites. Memory divided into four degrees : 1. Memory of the ſuits ; 2. of the honours ; 3. of the ſmall trumps ; and 4. of the ſmall cards.—Reaſons for rejecting artificial memory.—Wonderful memory of an old man.

Memoria————excolendo————augetur.

QUINTILIAN.

THIS curious game when firſt a novice tries,
He wonders where its difficulty lies :
The cards are all arrang'd in order due,
And its peculiar phraſes are but few :
Not like thoſe terms which might a volume fill,          5
The jargon of Piquette, or cramp Quadrille ;
Where *point* and *ſequence, tierces* and *quatorze,*
*Spadille, manillio, baſto, matadores,*
And twenty more exotic words combin'd
Perplex the ear, and ſtupify the mind.          10
But honeſt Whiſt, with native graces crown'd,
Diſdains the foppery of foreign ſound ;
And for a thouſand rules preſcribes but one,
*To make of ev'ry card the moſt you can.*

But

But let fuch poor, fuch fhallow reas'ners know, 15
What feems the eafieft is not always fo :
Whene'er the trial comes, they foon fhall find
That their ideas muft be much refin'd,
And many a maxim fink into their mind,
Ere from their groffeft errors they be cur'd,    20
And play fo well as ev'n to be endur'd.
'Tis thus with Xenophon's and Tully's ftyle,
As fweet as honey, and as fmooth as oil ;
'Tis thus with Addifon, our moral guide,
And gay Voltaire, the Gallic profe's pride :    25
Their art without furprife the reader fees,
And toil and ftudy takes for carelefs eafe ;
* Perfection's arduous fteep he deems a plain,
And fondly fancies his unpractis'd brain,

---

\* —————————Ut fibi quivis
Speret idem : fudet multum, fruftraque laboret
Aufus idem.—————

HORACE, IN ARTE POETICA, 240.

Cicero quodam loco fcribit, id effe optimum, quod cum te fa-
cilè credideris confequi imitatione, non poffis.

QUINTILIAN, l. xi. c. 1.

Without

Without refearch  (were he inclin'd to try)    30
Could equal happinefs of phrafe fupply.

 The man who wifhes well at Whift to play,
To three propitious pow'rs muft homage pay :
To Mem'ry firft, whofe faithful mirror clear
Before our fight bids all the paft appear ;    35
To Judgment next, whofe lamp's unerring ray
Guides thro' the mazes of the doubtful way ;
To Temper laft, whofe cool and wholefome breeze
From noxious mifts the mind's horizon frees.

 Queen of the fhadowy paft, to thee belong    40
The firft exertions of didactic fong.
Thine is the magic wand, whofe potent fway
Recalls its faded forms in juft array.
Each art from thee, divine, hiftoric maid,
And ev'ry fcience, borrows pow'rful aid ;    45
Nor could that fcience robb'd of thee fubfift,
Which yields to none of all the num'rous lift,
The fplendid fcience of delightful Whift.

G

The queen of cities, whofe immortal name
Yet fills the mouth of univerfal fame,                    50
Imperial Rome (as antiquarians fay)
Was not begun and finifh'd in a day.
And well we know that there was once a time,
When he who now on learning's height fublime
Commands Parnaffus with defpotic fway,              55
Could fcarcely ftammer out the letter A.
Let no one then henceforth prefume to fay
That he fhall never learn at Whift to play;
Or think, becaufe his memory is bad,
That one much better is not to be had.                 60
What floth muft dictate fuch a poor pretence!
What fhameful want of courage and of fenfe!
The fons of hope are heaven's peculiar care;
Whilft life remains 'tis impious to defpair.
For he who now, with all his pow'rs combin'd,      65
Can fcarce one moment keep the trumps in mind,
May climb at length perfection's lofty tree,
And play the game as well as Hoyle, or me.

                                                        The

The taſk at firſt appears not mighty hard,
To keep in mind the fate of ev'ry card ;                    70
Since ev'ry card, when play'd with quickneſs due,
In two ſhort minutes paſſes in review ;
And one ſhould think, that ev'n the weakeſt brain
So long with eaſe might ev'ry trace retain.
\* And yet how few, how very few we ſee,             75
That reach in this perfection's laſt degree !
Ev'n I, who play ſo oft the ſtudious game,
And like it better than I care to name ;
Ev'n I, bewilder'd in a maze of doubt,
At times forget how many trumps are out ;        80
When wayward fancy leads my thoughts aſtray,
To love, or verſe, or ſome ſuch idle way.
  Is it not then from this example clear,
That ſtrict attention is the virtue here ?

——————— Pauci, quos æquus amavit
Jupiter, aut ardens evexit ad æthera virtus,
Dis geniti, potuere.

VIRGIL, ÆNEID, vi. 129.

G 2

On

On which alone  (whatever floth pretends)          85
The whole great art of memory depends :
From which disjoin'd, the moft retentive brain
That ever nature gave, is giv'n in vain ;
But which poffeffing, in a length of days
The moft forgetful may afpire to praife.          90
   · Let all who fit them down at Whift to play,
From foreign objects turn their eyes away ;
And to the verdant board's illumin'd round
Their fears, their profpects, and their wifhes bound.
Let vulgar cares that inftant be refign'd,          95
  And vulgar paffions banifh'd from the mind :
There let the cit his golden views forget,
  And the poor bankrupt drop his load of debt :
There let the bard his rage for rhyming lofe,
And meditate no more the thanklefs mufe :          100
Let Flavia there her artful plans forfake,
Nor count the conquefts fhe intends to make :
Let Harpax there forget th' approaching treat,
Nor  unt the difhes he intends to eat:

                                        There

There let the recklefs youth, who weds to-morrow,

And buys his pleafures with an age of forrow,  106

From eager thoughts abftract his mental fight,

And pant no longer for the bridal night :

There let the haplefs youth, who hangs* to-morrow,

Drop for a while his penitence and forrow ;  110

From anxious feelings turn his eyes away,

And fhrink no longer from the public day.

But left in fancy's maze we rove too long,

To ftricter method let us call the fong ;

And fince we thus fo evidently find  115

That conftant practice, with attention join'd,

Will ftrengthen by degrees the weakeft mind,

Proceed we now to fhew by what degrees

The progrefs may be made with greateft eafe.

———————It goth by deftenye
To hange or wed ; both hath one houre ;
And whether it be, I am well fure
Hangynge is better of the twayne ;
Sooner done, and fhorter payne.
SCOLE HOWSE, 1542.

Let

Let each new votary at mem'ry's fhrine        120
His firft attention to the *fuits* confine,
In quick fucceffion as they rife to view,
And paint the board with red or fable hue.
Let him obferve from whom they firft proceed,
And mark the fate of each peculiar lead ;        125
If royal cards by vulgar trumps be won,
And by what hand the daring deed was done :
So fhall he ftill thofe adverfe fuits avoid,
Which give advantage to the hoftile fide ;
So fhall he ftill difcern his partner's mind,        130
And feldom fail his ftrength at home to find ;
So fhall he ne'er, at fome oblivious time,
Be charg'd with that unpardonable crime,
Which Paffion's eye with darkeft fury views,
And Patience ev'n herfelf can fcarce excufe—        135
The crime of fending to the hoftile fhore
The fame unlucky bark that fplit before ;
Or, when he fees his friend a fuit refufe,
Of failing to affift his cruel views.

So

So much for leſſon firſt ; whoſe height to gain

Is ſcarce too arduous for an infant brain ;  141

And yet infallible in which to be

Confers in mem'ry's ſchool no mean degree ;

But one with which full many reſt content,

Who half their ſtupid lives at Whiſt have ſpent. 145

But let not this with pride inflame your mind :

Think only what a taſk remains behind ;

See from the pack how each peculiar card

Impatient ſtarts, and claims your next regard ;

In number equal to the weeks, that here  150

In rings of Jewiſh work divide the year.

When firſt a ſtudent (whether old or young)

Sees in a Lexicon* ſome foreign tongue,

So many words to ev'ry letter fall,

He thinks no mem'ry can contain them all.  155

But when that regular and rigid maid,

Pedantic Grammar, lends her pow'rful aid,

---

* Lexicon, a poetical phraſe for a dictionary.

     And

And from the mafs of words affigns to each
Its proper rank among the parts of fpeech;
With eager joy he then his error fees,                    160
And learning's lofty ladder mounts with eafe.
And thus at Whift the party-colour'd crew,
Which ftrikes with fuch defpair the hafty view,
In mem'ry's eye will lefs terrific be,
By fkill divided into fquadrons three;                    165
Where *honours* firft, then *vulgar trumps* appear,
And bafe *plebeian cards* bring up the rear.

  And firft, the band of honour'd chiefs appears,
In number equal to the Scottifh peers;
Who not, like ours, from an illuftrious race            170
In Britain's fenate take their deftin'd place;
But, like the meaneft of the burgher train,
By vile dependent votes their feats obtain.

  O'er cards like thefe to fix her firm command,
Will not from mem'ry much of toil demand;                175
So much their gaudy forms attract the view,
And fuch effects their pow'rful fteps purfue.

                                        This

This point obtain'd, you need no farther go,
Of ev'ry fuit the reigning pow'rs to know;
And whether thofe yourfelf have kept in ftore  180
Are ftill as feeble as they were before;
Or if they now can march, in bold array,
Triumphant forth, and fweep the tricks away.
Ne'er fhall you then a guarded monarch fend,
From fome fell ace to meet his fruitlefs end;  185
Nor, when in rank of play you fecond ftand,
Permit a guarded queen to quit your hand,
Till fummon'd by the third, concluding round,
Or till both ace and king their fates have found.

Now to the *vulgar trumps*, in number nine,  190
Our whole attention let us next confine;
That fo with certainty we ftill may know
How far in ftrength we overmatch the foe;
And ne'er permit him, when our hand is in,
With an inferior trump a trick to win.  195
But fhould we find, when we have drawn the reft,
That our poor trump is but the fecond-beft,

So

So fhall we ftill the firft occafion take

Of fuch a trembling card a trick to make.

But fome, who think of Whift they fomething

know,                                          200

Will here refufe another ftep to go ;

And now to mem'ry's voice attend no more,

Since here her *ufeful* leffons all are o'er ;

And that uncommon reach of ample mind,

Where all the *vulgar cards* a ftation find,      205

Down from the ten inclufive to the deuce,

But very feldom will be found of ufe.

But thofe that entertain fuch narrow views,

Muft here the freedom of my fpeech excufe,

If I affert (whatever fkill they claim)           210

They are as yet but pupils in the game ;

For no good player deems the fmalleft card

That meets the board unworthy his regard ;

Since well he knows that ev'n the paltry deuce,

By art and judgment, may be turn'd to ufe.        215

Nor

Nor is there in the whole extent of play
A brighter gleam of rapture's golden ray,
Than his, whom Whist with genuine spirit fires,
Whene'er in this he gains his full desires;
When in the harmless house no trumps remain, 220
Or none at least that will his course restrain;
And forth he pours, with exultation mute,
The weakest children of his darling suit;
And from the foes, who scarce their temper keep,
Continues still the careless tricks to sweep; 225
Till ev'ry card be spent; and, last of all,
In vain reserv'd, their useless honours fall.
One trick, when seiz'd in this triumphant style,
Rewards with more delight the player's toil,
And is by him with far more joy survey'd, 230
Than half a score by kings and aces made.

When these *plebeian cards* together join,
They make three times the sacred number nine;
But think not therefore their extent to gain,
A task too arduous for a common brain. 235

Divifion here again his aid will lend,
And make your fteps with gradual eafe defcend,
Or (if you better like the phrafe) afcend.

Three ftately tens the long proceffion lead ;
Nines, eights, and fev'ns, and fixes next fucceed ; 240
Then fives, and fours, and trays ; till frequent ufe
At laft acquaint you with the humble deuce ;
Which, tho' the meaneft of the painted train,
Is here the pinnacle of mem'ry's fane.

But ere from mem'ry's fchool we fet you free,   245
Two more important points muft mention'd be ;
Which fome, who are in fkill furpafs'd by few,
At times will fuffer to efcape their view :
The point of knowing, when the hand is o'er,
How many *honours* either fide can fcore ;              250
And that which gives to mem'ry's full command
The royal cards turn'd up on either hand :
'Twere lofs of time the former's ufe to tell,
Nor on the latter need we long to dwell ;

Since

Since all will grant, in ev'ry common cafe, 255
To play were madnefs in an *honour*'s face;
And that to lead thro' trumps of high degree,
The firft of duties muft for ever be.

But fome will wonder, that, tho' here the mufe
On mem'ry's chapter has been thus diffufe, 260
She has not yet the flighteft mention made
Of that contrivance to afford her aid,
Her load to lighten, and abridge her toil,
Found by the genius of immortal Hoyle*;
By which arrangement's artful methods try 265
The want of recollection to fupply;
And each event that paffes on the board
Engage by diff'rent fymbols to record.
But I muft venture here to quit my guide,
And, urg'd by reafon, for myfelf decide, 270

⁊ See Hoyle, chap. xxi. inntled, An Artificial Memory, or
ar Eafy Method of affifting the Memory of thofe that play at
the Game of Whift

Whofe

Whose faithful voice, by mighty names unfway'd,
Condemns the impotence of foreign aid;
And loudly calls on ev'ry manly mind,
Its beft refources in itfelf to find.
Oh, be not then, ye pupils of my mufe,              275
Induc'd by floth fuch dang'rous aids to ufe :
Seek not on bladders weak as thefe to fail,
Whofe falfe affurance muft fo often fail;
But plunge with boldnefs in, all help difown,
And to your native vigour truft alone;              280
When perfevering labour's years are paft,
Secure to reach perfection's port at laft.

* A man of burgher blood I chanc'd to know,
Whofe head was white with fourfcore winters' fnow;
His frame was weaken'd by the weight of years, 285
And blunting deafnefs had affail'd his ears;

---

* I chanc'd an old Corycian fwain to know.
                    DRYDEN'S GEORGICS, iv. 188.

    Namque fub Oebaliæ memini me turribus altis,
    Quà niger humectat flaventia culta Galefus,
    Corycium vidiffe fenem.
                    VIRGIL, GEORG. iv. 125.

But

But ftill with keeneft glance his eagle eye
Could all that pafs'd upon the board defcry;
And daily practice, and inceffant thought,
Had mem'ry's pow'r to fuch perfection brought, 290
That not a deuce from any quarter fell,
But he thro' all the hand its fate could tell.
Accept, thou hoary fage, this feeble praife,
Which now to thee thy grateful pupil pays:
If he of fkill can boaft a decent fhare, 295
And plays his cards with tolerable care,
Be all the glory thine, whofe precepts kind
Enlarg'd his knowledge, and his views refin'd;
And whofe example firft his fpirit fir'd,
And emulation's ardour firft infpir'd; 300
Who taught him firft (whate'er the pedant fays)
That fkill at Whift confers no vulgar praife;
And that the man who could not play it well
(Howe'er he might in other arts excel) 304
To each politer fcene muft bid at once farewell.

As there are many people who are fonder of Truth when fhe appears in the humble fimplicity of profe, than when fhe is decked out in the trappings of poetry, the author thought it might not be amifs, at the end of this and the two following cantos (which are the only didactic parts of the work), to fubjoin the principal maxims they contain, in the fober habiliment of profaic plainnefs. The Appendix to the eighth and ninth cantos will naturally fall into the form of a commentary: but the prefent, being but half didactic, will only fupply a few practical axioms,

I. Never return the adverfaries' lead. v. 128.—An exception to this rule you will find in Canto IX. 66.

II. Always return your partner's lead. v. 130.

III. Never lead to the adverfaries' *ruff*. v. 136.

IV. Always return your partner's *ruff*, when you fee that he plays for it. v. 138.—See Canto IX. v. 52.

V. When you know that you hold the beft of two trumps, never fail to draw the other. v. 194.

VI. But when you know that yours is the worft, never lofe an opportunity of trumping with it. v. 196.

VII. Never play in the face of an *honour*. v. 256.

VIII. Always play through an *honour*. v. 257.

# W H I S T.

## C A N T O VIII.

II

## ARGUMENT.

Judgment, the second requisite at Whist.—Rules under this head almost innumerable.—First, of the duties of the leading hand.—Doctrine of trumps, and of the strong suit.

BUT much as Whist on mem'ry's pow'r depends,
You must not think that there the labour ends;
For were it thus, the man who knew it most
Could but the merit of a school-boy boast.
A far superior pow'r his aid must join,                    5
And make the charming science quite divine;
Unerring Judgment, whose supreme command
In ev'ry nicer case directs the hand.
But here so wide a prospect meets the sight,
That ev'n my daring muse recoils with fright:      10
So many points for her attention call,
She knows she never can dispatch them all.
As well might she attempt to reckon o'er
Each grain of sand on Ocean's founding shore,

Each

Each flow'r whofe beauty paints the vernal ground,
Each ftar that glitters in the azure round；　　　16
Or, dyed in glofly jet, each filken thread,
Whofe rich profufion decks my charmer's head.
For this good caufe it is her fage defign
To fome few rules her leffons to confine；　　　20
Whofe great importance is by all confefs'd,
And then to time and practice leave the reft.

　　The various duties of each diff'rent hand,
Arrang'd in order as at firft they ftand,
Or as they fhift about in courfe of play,　　　25
The fkilful verfe fhall now at large difplay.

　　On him, who, feated by the Dealer's fide,
Enjoys his privilege with confcious pride,
Firft from the barrier's bound to ftart away,
And open to the reft the lifts of play—　　　30
On him all eyes with fixt attention wait,
And trembling hope to fee the birth of fate.

　·　A youth juft ent'ring on the ftage of life,
And keen to ftruggle in preferment's ftrife,

　　　　　　　　　　　　　　　　By

By one rafh ftep may hurt his fortune more 35
Than all his future prudence can reftore.
Thus will it fare with him whofe want of heed
Sets off at firft with fome imprudent lead;
His influence loft he never may regain,
But oft his overfight lament in vain; 40
Whofe dire effect may give the foe command,
And fpoil the profpects of the faireft hand.
Stop then, my fon, and, ere thy card defcend,
Reflect how much may on its fate depend;
Nor venture thus, by rafh and wanton play, 45
The hopes of two at once to caft away.

 Firft then, with careful eye your force review,
And range the various *fuits* in order due;
Confider next, amid the painted throng,
If your appointed band of trumps be ftrong; 50
Since to begin with them, whene'er you can,
Is (tho' the boldeft) ftill the fafeft plan;
For nought can here fuch want of fkill betray,
Or give fuch evidence of wretched play,

As

As when of trumps you hold a decent fhare,        55
To keep them prifon'd up with cow'rdly care,
Till they at laft their forc'd appearance make,
At times conftrain'd your partner's *tricks* to take.

Some afk why women here fo oft go wrong,
And like to keep them in their hands fo long ?        60
To me the caufe of this was always plain ;
They love to keep th' authority they gain.

When firft in queft of trumps you fearch your
        hand,
Should five, or more than five, in waiting ftand,
Oh, do not then one precious moment lofe,        65
To draw the reft their envied pow'r to ufe.
What tho' your other cards are all fo poor
That they one fingle trick can fcarce enfure ;
Remember ftill (nor keep, with felfifh mind,
Your whole attention to yourfelf confin'd)        70
How much your fending thus the trumps away
May chance to benefit your partner's play ;

                                Remember

Remember too, the weaker you may be,
For ftrength of cards the greater chance has he.

But if, turn'd up, a trump of high command      75
In threat'ning attitude againft you ftand,
You then had better change your mode of play,
And (for a time at leaft) the trumps delay.
Until your partner chance the lead to gain,
With patience wait—nor fhall you wait in vain; 80
For he who trumps can lead with greater eafe,
Will fure for that the firft occafion feize,
While you behind the foe fecure remain,
And thus your point with lefs of danger gain.

But now perhaps of trumps you hold but four,
And yet of cards can boaft a decent ftore;        86
If with thefe cards you *tricks* intend to win,
Prevent renounces, and with trumps begin.
And yet from lefs than four you muft not lead,
Unlefs your hand of cards be great indeed.       90

But here obferve, that fhould your trumps be three,
And each of thefe an *honour* chance to be;

Knave,

Knave, queen, and king; or king, with queen and
    ace;
It will be then a very diff'rent cafe;
For cards like thefe, of fuch fupreme command,  95
You ne'er fhould keep one moment in your hand;
But fend them forth the meaner troops to draw,
To fweep the board, and keep the world in awe.
But knave and queen, when with an ace conjoin'd,
Will thrive much better when at home confin'd, 100
For reafons good; which if you wifh to know,
Attempt to guefs, or feek them out below*.

But when your hand for its appointed fhare
Of pow'rful trumps receives a royal pair,
Your play will then demand peculiar care:   105
Since this, when all the diff'rent pairs you take,
No lefs than fix varieties will make;
From three of which you ne'er fhould fail to lead,
Tho' fome than others better will fucceed;

* See below, at verfe 231.

Ace,

Ace, king the beft ; then king with queen conjoin'd,

While queen and knave muft follow far behind. 111

And yet this pair a better chance will have,

Than knave with king, or ev'n than ace and knave.

But (far the worft of all the royal band)

Allow not ace and queen to quit your hand.         115

On this, however, at another time

* We mean to lavifh greater length of rhyme.

   Whene'er of honour'd chiefs you hold but one,

To fend him forth is ftill the fafeft plan.

Let then your ace, of trumps difpatch a round ;    120

For him no better ufe could e'er be found.

And ev'n the other chiefs, of lefs degree,

Will thus by far of more advantage be ;

While from the foe they force fupreme command,

And ferve to ftrengthen too your partner's hand. 125

   But fhould your lucklefs hand ftill weaker be,

And hold but one poor trump of low degree,

* See below, at verfe 231.

                                        With

With which you mark but little chance to *ruff*,

To play it out may oft do well enough ;

For then your partner will the lead return,          130

And thus to good account your weaknefs turn ;

While he purfues your but-commencing plan,

And takes at ev'ry round two trumps for one.

But this, altho' at times it fhould be done,

At other times 'twere better far to fhun ;          135

For you may judge it will not always do,

So foon your weaknefs to expofe to view.

   For making trumps the firft commencing round

Another reafon good may ftill be found ;

Which, tho' but half deriv'd from Judgment's fchool,

Has yet the force of univerfal rule ;          141

That when you know not well what elfe to play,

To lead from trumps is ftill the fafeft way ;

As that great fuit (howe'er it chance to fall)

Can hurt your partner's hand the leaft of all.          145

   So much for trumps—whofe doctrine to explain,

With more than common labour racks the brain :

But

But which to know, profeffors all agree
The moſt important point at Whiſt to be.

But when from trumps debarr'd, without diſpute,
The next beſt lead is from the ſtrongeſt ſuit ;    151
Not from that ſuit which higheſt cards can boaſt,
But ſtill from that whoſe number counts the moſt.
And here the player of ſupreme degree
Will from the novice beſt diſtinguiſh'd be ;    155
Who early *tricks* is anxious ſtill to take,
And ev'ry king and ace at firſt to make ;
As if the cards which once dominion gain,
The fame ſuperior pow'r could not retain.
But he who plays with more extenſive views,    160
A widely diff'rent courſe from this purſues ;
And ſtrives of ev'ry ſuit within his hand
As long as poſſible to keep command.
From four, and five, and ſix, and deuce, and tray,
Will he much rather than from *honours* play :    165
For theſe, tho' now ſo weak and poor they be,
He hopes in time of greater force to ſee :

But

But cautious ftill, he wifhes firft to know

Of this beft fuit what cards his friend can fhew ;

Whofe ftrength if there he likewife find to lie,   170

To draw the trumps he boldly means to try,

That when at laft their fuit's oppofers fall,

Without difturbance they may make them all.

   But from the ftrongeft fuit if thus to lead,

Can only from fuperior fkill proceed,        175

What words will ferve our cenfure to convey

Of thofe who always from their weakeft play !

Who, when of any fuit they hold but one,

With ftupid rapture hug the darling plan,

That one immediate from their hand to fpurn,   180

And eager wait to trump its next return !

What folly muft infpire the wretched tafte,

So many precious trumps on *ruffs* to wafte !

With what fell weapons of indignant rage

Shall I this vile, pernicious pow'r engage,      185

Which leads fo far from judgment's paths aftray,

And combats ev'ry rule of wholefome play ?

                             Not

Not for this purpofe has indulgent Heav'n
Such ftrength of trumps to favour'd mortals giv'n :
That very trump you madly caft away,                190
Might have in time obtain'd imperial fway ;
From all offence your better fuits fecur'd,
And three good *tricks* befides its own procur'd

But fhould your fortune be fo very low,
That *ruffs* are all the hope your hand can fhew,    195
Remember ftill that it is dang'rous play,
Thus at the firft your weaknefs to betray ;
And tho' a *ruff* would fuit your lucklefs ftate,
At leaft with patience for its coming wait ;
Nor be like thofe who ftill impatient fit,           200
To wound their comrades with the darts of wit ;
While wit that lacks occafion's fair excufe,
Muft much of force, and much of beauty lofe.

If no ftrong fuit, on which your hopes to place,
Your fate affords, in that unlucky cafe,             205
The next beft lead is from a king and ace.

But

But if my counsel you will here obey,
I would not have you both at once to play ;—
Make but one step—no farther then proceed,
But try your partner on another lead :     210
So shall you keep the suit's command ; and so
Your friend instructed shall hereafter know
In what good quarter sits your fairest wind,
And still be sure your strength at home to find.

   Next to the suit, where ace and king are join'd,
The suits of each apart you best will find ;     216
For if you here with some small card begin,
Your partner's queen may chance a *trick* to win ;
But if one card alone your king defend,
Be ne'er induc'd that card abroad to fend ;     220
For very seldom will the ace be found
To leave his palace the commencing round.

   From king and queen is but a sorry lead,
And will be found but seldom to succeed ;
For both conjoin'd, if either first advance,     225
To make two *tricks* have but a slender chance ;

                             And,

And, if you fport a card of low degree,
The knave will probably the gainer be.

To lead from knave and ace, or king and knave,
I hope you feldom fhall occafion have.	230

But when a queen attends an ace's fide,
That worft of all the fuits with care avoid;
At leaft till fate a better lead refufe,
And of two evils force the leaft to choofe.
And thus to wait you muft not reckon hard,	235
Since patience here will be its own reward;
For if upon the left that fuit begin,
Then both your ace and queen are fure to win:
But fhould your friend, or on the right your foe,
Attempt that fuit, then on your queen muft go; 240
Ev'n then you have the chance of two to one,
To make them both by this advent'rous plan.

I told you once, as you remember may,
* Of trumps a fingle *honour* ftill to play;

* See above, at verfe 118.

Let it be knave, or queen, or king, or ace ;        245
But other suits make quite a diff'rent case :
To keep them up is here the better plan ;
A single ace will still command the clan ;
And ev'n the rest, if they in hand remain,
Have still some slender chance their *tricks* to gain.

But now the suit is fix'd—what single card        251
Of each to play demands your next regard ;—
An easy point, on which my hasty song
Conceives it needless to detain you long ;
For that the lowest still should first appear,        255
Admits but only one exception here.
Of *sequence*, upwards from the number three,
Be sure to lead the highest in degree ;
Which to your partner, if he bear a brain*,
Will still the nature of your hand explain,        260
And save his better cards from being spent in vain.

* Nay, I do bear a brain.
  SHAKESPEAR's ROMEO AND JULIET, Act 1, Sc. 4.

How

How bleft is he, who can, when elder hand,
With reafon hope to gain the game's command ;
Who ftrength of trumps with joyful eye beholds,
And of each other fuit the tenace holds !        265
He fearlefs ftill can with his trumps begin,
Nor cares he much what hand the *trick* may win ;
Secure of this, where'er the lead remain,
That he his former pow'r fhall foon regain.

I        COMMEN-

___

## COMMENTARY on CANTO VIII.

### DUTIES OF THE LEADING HAND.

Query 1. What suit to lead?

Answer. Lead always trumps when you can. v. 51.

### DOCTRINE OF TRUMPS. 63 to 145.

Lead always from five or more trumps, however weak your hand of cards may be, unless an honour be turned up against you. 63 to 84.—HOYLE, chap. i. rule 2.

Lead from four trumps with a tolerable hand. 85 to 88.

You must not lead trumps from less than four, unless in the two following cases:

I. If your hand of cards be very great. 90.

II. If your trumps be honours.

Of three honours, lead always from ace, king, and queen; or king, queen, and knave: but not from ace, queen, and knave. v. 91 to 102.

Of two honours, lead always with ace and king, king and queen, and even queen and knave; but seldom with ace and knave, or king and knave; and never with ace-queen. v. 103 to 117.

Lead always with a single honour, whatever it be; which serves to strengthen your partner's hand. v. 118 to 125.

Leading with a single small trump, with which you have no chance of ruffing, will not unfrequently be found eligible; as it

has

has the effect, when returned, of drawing two for one. The chief objection is, that it expofes rather too foon the weaknefs of your hand. 126 to 137.

There is ftill another reafon for leading trumps; when you have no other good fuit; trumps being always the leaft dangerous lead. 138 to 145.

### DOCTRINE OF THE STRONG SUIT. 150 to 204.

The next eligible lead to trumps, is your ftrongeft fuit; not that of which you have the beft, but that of which you have the moft cards. Bad players are anxious to make their great cards at firft, as if they would not be good at any time. Good ones, on the contrary, wifh to keep the command of a fuit as long as they poffibly can. By playing from your ftrongeft fuit, you have always the chance of making a trick or two on it at the end of the hand; and you difcover, at the fame time, how your partner ftands with regard to it, and whether it will be worth while to play trumps on its account. v. 150 to 173.

But if playing from the ftrongeft fuit be thus eligible, how foolifh and abfurd muft be the conduct of thofe who always chufe to play from the weakeft, and who never are happy but when fifhing for a ruff! Befides the danger of expofing their weaknefs, they thus wafte thofe precious trumps, which were intended for a very different purpofe. Even if your hand be fo low that a ruff is almoft your only hope, you fhould at leaft wait with patience till it come. 174 to 203.

---

Next to a ftrong fuit is one with ace and king; but you fhould ftop after playing one of them, and try your partner with another

lead;

lead; who will thus know afterwards where to find you at home.
204 to 214.

Next to the fuit of ace and king together, is that in which they
are each apart. By leading a fmall card from either, your partner
has a chance of making the queen if he has her. But if your
king be but once guarded, avoid that as a very dangerous lead.
215 to 222.

King and queen is but a bad lead; for if you begin with either
of them, you may chance to make but one trick of the fuit; and
if you lead a fmall one, you will moft probably give one to the
knave. 223 to 228.

King and knave is alfo a bad lead. 229-30.

But of all the leads ace and queen is the worft; which therefore fhould be avoided as long as you can : for if it is led to you
from the left hand, you cannot fail to make them both; and even
fhould the fuit be begun by either of the other two players, by
venturing your queen the firft round, your chance for two tricks is
not inconfiderable. 231 to 242.

Never lead with a fingle honour of any fuit except trumps;
for even a guardlefs king, queen, or knave, when kept up, have
fome chance of making a trick. 243 to 250.

———————

Query II. What particular card of the fuit to lead?
Anfwer. In general the loweft; but where you have fe-
quence of three or more, then always begin with the higheft.
251 to 261. See HOYLE, chap. xiv.

.

# W H I S T.

## CANTO IX.

## ARGUMENT.

Judgment continued.—Duties of him who recovers the lead.—Duties of the fecond in hand. Of the third, including the doctrine of finessing.—Duties of the last in hand.—Doctrine of calling, and of playing by the stages of the game.

BUT tho', when once a hand is well begun,
Half of the player's tafk, and more, is done;
Yet muft he never think of paufing there,
But watch its progrefs with unceafing care;
And when his luck obtains the lead anew,                    5
His former plans with vigour ftill purfue.

If trumps to play be firft expedient found,
Then let him now difpatch another round;
And ftill more keenly urge the daring plan,
When he has hopes of taking two for one.                   10
But fhould in trumps a diff'rent fate prevail,
And not his partner, but his foe fhould fail,
'Twere better then to change his mode of play,
And (for a time at leaft) his fcheme delay.

                                                          But

But if his hand of cards be great indeed,          15
At all adventures let him then proceed;
And, rather than his fuits were kept in awe,
Rifque from his friend the laft of trumps to draw.
But when two trumps alone remain behind,
Should he the higheft ftill againft him find,          20
From his ftrong fuit fome potent card to play,
May chance to force it from the field away.
And here the fame deliv'rance to produce,
A thirteenth card will oft be found of ufe,

The lead of trumps was not at firft your view,   25
But fome ftrong fuit—then ftill that fuit purfue;
By which, when doubt and danger's hour is paft,
You oft a *trick* or two may catch at laft.

But fhould you fail in ev'ry darling plan,
And fhould your wretched hand afford not one,   30
Be then content a fecond part to play,
And yield entirely to your partner's fway;
To him alone your whole attention turn,
And ftill, whene'er you can, his leads return.

But

But if he twice has led, nor both the fame,  35
Still let the firſt* your firſt obſervance claim;
Leſt from the next you ſhould receive a bite,
And find it was involuntary quite.

But more than all, that worſt of faults avoid,
Which ev'n to wrath might move a ſtoic's pride;  40
When your friend's cyes with keen impatience
     burn,
From all the houſe the hoſtile trumps to turn,
Inſtead of trumps, his weakneſs† to return.
For the poor torch, that burns at either end,
To ruin's dreary gulph muſt ſoon defcend;  45
And ev'n the ſtrongeſt hand will ſoon decay,
When both conſtrain'd to trump, and trumps to play.

And yet you muſt not think at ev'ry time,
To lead your partner's *ruff*, a mortal crime;

---

* You are to make a wide difference between a lead of choice
and a forced lead of your partner's.

HOYLE, chap. xii. art. 3.

† His *weakneſs*, poetically, for his weak fuit.

For

For I can cafes four before you lay,                    50

In all of which it is the beft of play.

When from his conduct you can clearly fee

That fuch a ftep will acceptable be :

Or when yourfelf a pow'r of trumps can boaft,

And ere your rage attacks the rival hoft,              55

Your eyes for him a likely chance furvey,

With one or two of his to fteal away :

Or when you hope (the hope is here enough)

To treat his malice with an *over-ruff* :

Or laft of all, but higheft in degree,                 60

If fortune fhould fo favourable be,

In both your hands at once a *ruff* to place,

Fail not the *faw** that inftant to embrace ;

Which you fhall ftill of fuch advantage find,

That all your former plans were well refign'd.         65

 

    * Whenever you gain the advantage of eftablifhing of a *faw*,
it is your intereft to embrace it.

HOYLE, chap. viii.

But

But he whofe breaft a chriftian fpirit bears
No more at Whift than other great affairs,
Will ever choofe to keep, with felfifh mind,
His whole attention to his friends confin'd ;
Since (ftrange to tell) it may at times fucceed,    70
Ev'n to return your enemies their lead.
When he upon the right too weak is found
To raife his partner's firft commencing round,
So fhall that foe, the lead at firft who plann'd,  ⎫
Be forc'd at once to quit the fuit's command,    75 ⎬
Or with an eafy *trick* oblige your partner's hand.  ⎭
And yet this fcheme you never ought to try,
Unlefs your own no better lead fupply ;
For danger often waits that fuit's return,
And flighted weaknefs may to malice turn.    80
But having now difpatch'd the elder hand,
The fecond's duties next our care demand ;
Which as they ftand, the firft commencing round,
No very arduous tafk will fure be found ;

Since

Since all the secret then, without dispute,          85
Is but to play the worst of ev'ry suit.

  Yet in each gen'ral rule, however plain,
Some few exceptions there must still remain.
If both your hand contain, or king, or ace
Should shew without delay his honest face.          90

  Remember too, as you before* were told,
To play your queen, if ace and queen you hold.

  Yours is the king, and but one single card
By fate bestow'd the monarch's side to guard:
Let then his royal figure first advance,          95
Which still for safety is his fairest chance;
Tho' this too often proves a cruel case,
And leads him forth to meet the fatal ace.

  Put up, when guarded once, or queen or knave,
For both the fairest chance their lives to save.          100

  In all the following rounds, the second hand
Requires from judgment no precise command:

* See above, Canto VIII. 240.

                            Or

Or fhould the pupil afk a certain rule,

We then muft fend him back to mem'ry's* fchool.

   And yet, before we quite this chapter leave,   105

One ufeful caution let him firft receive:

When any fuit, of which his hand is out,

To trump or not to trump he ftands in doubt,

If he can caft a lofing card away,

To *pafs* the *trick* is always better play,       110

(Which ftill his partner has a chance to gain)

Than rifque the wafting of his trumps in vain.

   Nor think that here too great a length I go,

For one poor trump fuch anxious care to fhew;

For, were I urg'd fome fingle rule to find,      115

Where Whift's true effence moft fhould meet the

       mind,

My maxim fhould be ftill in fuch a cafe,

*A proper value on the trumps to place.*

   We taught forbearance to the fecond hand,

But give the third an oppofite command;     120

---

\* See above, Canto VII. 178—189.

                   And

And recommend to him the daring plan,

To play at ev'ry round the beft he can :

Unlefs the cards that meet his judging eye

Permit his fkill the fecond-beft to try ;

With queen and ace, to venture firft the queen,   125

And rifque the royal fire that lies between ;

With king and knave, to rifque the royal dame ;

With queen and ten, with knave and nine the fame.

Nor need we here much farther down to go,

Becaufe importance feldom dwells below.        130

   Such is the doctrine of fineffing's* art ;

A ftrong temptation to the daring heart ;

To which no *tricks* more pleafure can convey,

Than thofe obtain'd in this advent'rous way.

---

  * Fineffing, fays Hoyle, means the endeavouring to gain an
advantage by art and fkill, which confifts in this : when a card is
led, and you have the beft and third-beft card of that fuit, you
judge it beft to put your third-beft card upon that lead, and run
the rifque of your adverfary's having the fecond-beft of it; that
if he has it not, which is two to one againft him, you are then fure
of gaining a trick. Chap. xx.

And yet the danger it defies is fuch, 135
I fear it ought not to be practis'd much ;
Unlefs of trumps you boaft the full command,
Or have already quell'd the hoftile band :
And if your plan fucceeds, you then could claim
To fave your lurch, or reckon up the game. 140

But ftill remember this, my docile fon,
That you in trumps much greater rifques may run
Than with another fuit could well be done :
For trumps will ftill their native pow'r retain,
Nor can by other trumps be render'd vain. 145

The laft in hand has fure the eafieft plan ;
Only to catch whatever *tricks* he can.
And yet at times ev'n he might errors make,
And for a paltry *trick* his game forfake,
If, while fome trumps againft him ftill remain, 150
His own beft trump he thus fhould wafte in vain.

But fome will here, I know, with boldnefs fay,
" To pafs a *trick* is always wretched play."

And

And yet I will aſſert, in ſpite of ſuch,
That ev'n a *trick* at times may coſt too much ;   155
Should it from all reſtraint the foe relieve,
Or in your hand a guardleſs *honour* leave.
But oh, what words can paint the dire diſgrace,
The ſhameful crime, of trumping with an ace,
Until it loſe its relative degree,   160
And chance the ſole ſurviving trump to be !
As well might George, when he in ſtate appears,
Enthron'd with ſplendor in the Houſe of Peers,
Were ſome raſh knave ſo daring then to be,
As make with honourable pockets free ;   165
As well might he, whenc'er the fact was known,
Jump down indignant from his royal throne,
And ſeizing by the neck without delay,
Himſelf to Newgate haul the wretch away :
Nor would he thus a ſtranger figure cut,   170
Than ace of trumps to ſuch an office put.

   Sometimes the perſon who is laſt in hand
Is eager to obtain the lead's command.

That

That he may then purfue fome darling plan,

Which his friend can't, or will not if he can.     175

'Twere better far than thus to wait in vain,

To take at once his partner's trick again,

To rout the routed, and to flay the flain.

 Thus have we now difpatch'd the diff'rent hands,

And Calling's art fome notice next demands :     180

That right which thofe the point of eight that reach,

Have ftill to make invocatory fpeech ;

That when the one two honours holds in hand,

He fhould aloud his partner's aid demand ;

That fo their forces join'd may game fupply,     185

And all the rifque of adverfe *tricks* defy.

 But tho' a game may thus be gain'd with eafe,

The tempting chance you fhould not always feize ;

For how muft you the difappointment mourn,

Whene'er your queftion meets with no return !     190

How much would fuch a ftep your hand expofe

To all the malice of your cruel foes !

K

Let

Let ev'ry player then this pow'r decline,
Save at the adverfe points of four and nine;
The one to bar the *trick*'s uneven claim,                    195
The other to fecure a double game;
Unlefs in Scotia's land he chance to play,
Where I am told by fome, that trav'llers fay,
They have in playing Whift a diff'rent way.
That when the foes are *love*, or none at all,                200
To gain a triple game they always *call*.
That greedy race, who, for the love of gold,
In days of yore their lucklefs monarch fold;
Who ftill unchang'd, the fame defires obey,
And ev'n at Whift their avarice betray.                    205

    Now hear, before you part from Judgment's fchool,
The laft, but not the leaft important rule;
That ftill before you dare a card to play,
You with attention muft your fcore furvey;
And never fail to regulate your game,                    210
By what the nature of that fcore may claim.

                                        At

At diff'rent times the fame identic hand
Will diff'rent modes of management demand.
When firft you enter on the doubtful way,
You then fhould ftill with vent'rous courage play;
Then is the time with boldnefs to fineffe, 216
And for a greater good to rifque a lefs.
But when at laft you to the goal draw near,
A very diff'rent courfe you then fhould fteer;
By flow but certain fteps to conqueft creep, 220
And take no *trick* you are not fure to keep.

And here the price of long laborious years,
The end of all your toils at laft appears.
You now on fair perfection's fummit ftand,
And can with eafe the vulgar world command; 225
Secure of this, that but a very few
To fuch a height will e'er your fteps purfue.
For moft, enflav'd by floth's deftructive fway,
Advance no farther than the middle way;
Nor think, by reaching fuch exalted praife, 230
To what a glorious pitch they might their natures
raife.

Let

Let others still with admiration view
Pedantic learning's scientific crew ;
Whose eyes the secrets of the heav'ns explore,
Or found the depths of geometric lore ;—    235
Let them with wonder look on those that reign,
Or guide the havock of th' embattled plain ;
On those whose skill directs the helm of state,
Or sways at will the senate's fierce debate.
To me, nor study, senate, throne, nor field,    240
Of man's superior soul such proofs can yield,
As that dear place, the first in reason's eye,
Where Whist's professors meet their skill to try ;
Where order still her strictest pow'r maintains,
And almost universal silence reigns ;    245
Where great events on ev'ry moment wait,
And ev'ry motion is the stamp of fate :
While Judgment there, thro' each important hour,
Displays the triumphs of his godlike pow'r ;
And clearly shews to what a height refin'd,    250
Attention's force with perseverance join'd,
Above the vulgar crew can raise the human mind.

COMMENTARY on CANTO IX.

### DUTIES OF HIM WHO RECOVERS THE LEAD. v. 1—80.

He fhould pufh the trumps which he has already begun; efpecially if he thinks he fhall take two for one. The contrary fufpicion is the only reafon for making him difcontinue trumps:
but if he has a very great hand of cards, it will then be proper to
run all rifques; even that of drawing the laft trump from his
partner. But when there are only two trumps in the houfe, and
he finds that the beft is againft him, let him force it out with a
card of his ftrong fuit; even a thirteenth card is often ufeful
upon fuch an occafion. v. 7—24.

Next to the duty of pufhing trumps, is that of continuing your
ftrong fuit; by which you will probably make a trick or two at
laft. v. 25—28.

But if you find that you cannot accomplifh your plan, or if your
hand be fo poor that you have none to accomplifh, you muft then
be entirely fubfervient to your partner, and lofe no opportunity of
returning his leads; but if he has led to you from two fuits, be
fure to give always the preference to the firft, as the other may
probably have only been forced. Above all, never lead to his
ruff, when you have reafon to imagine that he wifhes for trumps:
but more efpecially if he has played for them. There are indeed
only four cafes in which you fhould lead to your partner's re-
nounce: 1. When you fee that he exprefsly defires it. 2. When

you

you are very ftrong in trumps, and wifh, before you begin to draw
them from the enemy, to give him an opportunity of making one
of his. 3. When you think that he has a chance of an over-
ruff. And 4. When you can eftablifh between you a fee-faw,
which is fo advantageous, that every other plan fhould be re-
nounced to embrace it. v. 29—65.

When the right-hand adverfary is unable to raife his partner's
lead, it will be very proper for you to return it, as it will give your
partner an opportunity of making a trick cheaply, or force from
your left-hand adverfary the command of the fuit. This, however, fhould never be preferred to a good lead, either of your own
or your partner's, efpecially as there is frequently a rifque of the
right-hand adverfary trumping that fuit. v. 66—80.

---

### DUTIES OF THE SECOND HAND.  v. 81—118.

Thefe at firft are a very eafy matter, being only playing always
the worft of the fuit; except, 1. When he has ace and king; in
which cafe one of them muft be played. 2. When he has ace and
queen; where the queen fhould be put on. 3. When his king
is but once guarded, where he ought always to put him on; as
the chance is, that the fuit was led from an ace. 4. When either
his queen or knave happens to be but once guarded; in which
cafe, putting them up is almoft their only chance for a trick.
v. 81—100.

When a fuit is led, of which he has none, and he is doubtful
whether to trump it or not; if he has a lofing card to throw away,

it

it will generally be the better play to pass it, especially as there is a chance of its being taken by your partner. v. 105—112.

The most important of all maxims at Whist, is to set a proper value upon the trumps. 113—118.

---

## Duties of the Third Hand. v. 119—145.

The general rule is here the reverse of that of the second hand; being to put on the best of the suit. An exception to this is in the case of finessing, when you hold ace-queen, king-knave, queen-ten, knave-nine, or the like; and put on the lowest of the two cards, in hopes that the intermediate one lies not behind you. The temptation to finessing is very great, and yet it is such a dangerous practice, that it ought but rarely to be ventured, unless when you are very strong in trumps, and have a chance, by gaining the finessed trick, of saving your lurch, or of getting the game. Still, however, you may venture more in trumps than in any of the other suits.

---

## Duties of the Last Hand. v. 146—178.

These are in general the easiest of all, being only to take the trick if he can. And yet he should never, for the sake of a trick, part with the best trump in the house, or leave an honour guardless in his hand. But, above all, he should never trump with an ace, unless when it happens to be the last trump. v. 146—171.

It may sometimes be proper to take his partner's trick, when

K 4

he is very defirous o getting the lead, to execute any particular
project, which he fufpects that his partner either cannot, or will
not humour. v. 172—178.

---

### DOCTRINE OF CALLING.

This is rather a dangerous expedient ; as it runs a rifque, if un-
fuccefsful, of expofing the hand ; and ought therefore never to
be attempted, unlefs when the adverfaries are at nine, or upon the
eve of faving their lurch. v. 179—205.

### DOCTRINE OF PLAYING BY THE STAGES OF THE GAME. v. 206—221.

At the beginning of the game you fhould play with boldnefs ;
but when it comes near a clofe, with caution and forbearance.

# W H I S T.

## CANTO X.

# ARGUMENT.

Temper, the third requiſite at Whiſt.—Three cauſes of loſs of temper. 1. Bad luck. 2. Croſs play. And 3. A bad partner.—Cards, a terrible trial for the temper.—Story of Smilinda and her lover Puſillo.

What do you think it was all about ?——It was all about a game of
cards.                                             MURPHY.


THUS far the mufe has urg'd her daring toil,
Beneath the guidance of immortal Hoyle :
But here, alas ! his guardian pow'r is o'er,
His voice fhall animate the ftrain no more ;
Whofe efforts now muft his protection lofe,        5
And for themfelves another mafter choofe.

Come, then, thou fpirit, whofe delightful pow'r
Infpir'd fo late, in fancy's faireft hour,
Serena's bard ; and taught his liquid lays
* To reach the fplendid heights of Temper's praife ;
Come, then, and pour on me propitious too         11
Some precious drops of infpiration's dew ;

* Hayley, the author of the Triumphs of Temper.

6                              For

For I can juftly now thy favour claim,

Since now my fubject is with his the fame :

That fo the mufe, by thy affiftance ftrong,     15

May lead with eafe the tuneful ftream along,

And with redoubled vigour clofe the fong.

    In vain has Mem'ry's ftrength enlarg'd your

       mind,

In vain has Judgment's force your fkill refin'd,

Unlefs a third propitious pow'r be join'd.     20

For fhould you not with cooleft Temper play,

You muft be always in a lofing way ;

Since paffion ruffles and difturbs the mind,

And makes the keeneft judgment weak and blind ;

Ev'n mem'ry's mirror too, however fair,     25

It clouds, and fcatters all the traces there.

    * The ftorms which ruffle Temper's placid lake,

And oft on Whift fuch frightful havock make,

Diftort his features, and inflame his eyes,

From three important caufes take their rife.     30

* Che nel Lago del Cuor m'era durata.

           DANTE's INFERNO, c. i. 20.

· The

The firſt is *want of luck*, a pow'rful cauſe,
When fortune from your ſide entire withdraws;
And tho' invok'd the whole complaining night,
With ſcarce one decent hand will bleſs your ſight;
But ſtill goes on inverted knaves to ſend,                     35
Or aceleſs, faceleſs cards without an end.
And yet tho' this may ſeem a fair excuſe,
For weaker minds their temper's pow'r to loſe;
Ne'er do thou yield to paſſion's wild controul,
Nor let his influence warp thy firmer ſoul.                    40
But one poor trump your preſent cards contain,
And ſcarce an *honour* there, one *trick* to gain;
But let not then your looks of wild deſpair
This ſtate of weakneſs to the foes declare;——
Next hand may give you ſix, to make amends,                    45
And put four kings and aces in your friend's.
But ſhould your fate its malice ſtill purſue,
And bar from ev'ry hope your anxious view,
Get up, and ſmiling ſay, You'll play no more;
You won't be beaten till your bones are ſore;                  50

And

And rather fnatch the very worſt excuſe,
Than both your temper and your money loſe.

   Of temper's loſs, another cruel cauſe,
*Untoward play*, our next attention draws;
When all your kings and aces, as they riſe,    55 ⎱
Are ſeen, by turns, with horror and ſurpriſe    ⎰
In pieces cut before your angry eyes;
Or when, malignant fate's ſevereſt frown,
A dire *ſee-ſaw*, ſends all to ruin down;
And tho' you might with eaſe the foe reſtrain, 60 ⎱
Command's returning hour you wait in vain,    ⎰
And never till too late the lead regain.
And here, indeed, in this vexatious caſe,
I could at times excuſe a troubled face.
But let not ſtill each adverſe pow'r combin'd 65 ⎱
Rob you of that you muſt ſo uſeful find,    ⎰
The firm poſſeſſion of your manly mind.
For then perhaps your violent deſpair
May blunt the quickneſs of your wonted care;

                                          And

And while the mift of paffion blinds your views, 70
Some fair occafion you may chance to lofe
To check, tho' late, the crofs career of play,
And turn the fortunes of the doubtful day.

   Of caufes not the leaft, tho' laft in place,
Is that unlucky, crofs, provoking cafe,         75
When in an evil hour, yourfelf conjoin'd
With fome unfkilful wretch you chance to find;
With one perhaps who never look'd in Hoyle,
Or, if he did, who might have fpar'd the toil:
Who neither memory nor judgment fhews,       80
And of the plaineft rules who nothing knows:
Whofe thoughtlefs king, with firm undaunted face,
Comes frequent forth to meet the cruel ace;
And who, in fpite of warning, ftill proceeds
To play his foe's, and trump his partner's leads.    85
And here again, while fuch a caufe I view,
I could at times excufe a curfe or two.
But ftill remember, that on fuch a brain
The ftorm of paffion muft be fpent in vain;

                                        Or,

Or, what is worfe, the very pains you take      9●

May ftill more ftupid chance his mind to make;

May darken quite what was not clear before,

And from one blunder propagate a fcore.

Much better had you then fubmit to fate,

And ftill with patience your deliv'rance wait;      95

From his fupport all hopes at once refign,

And to yourfelf alone your thoughts confine;

Without complaint his groffeft faults endure,

And bear in filence what you cannot cure:

And this, when plac'd on fuch unlucky ground,      100

The fkilful player's mode will ftill be found;

Ev'n were he leagu'd with that illuftrious dame,

Of whofe nice judgment I have heard the fame;

To which her partner, when the hand was o'er,

In thefe emphatic words his witnefs bore:      105

" Of all the cards that thro' your fingers pafs'd,

" But one you play'd aright, and that the laft."

    Oft have I feen fome matrimonial dove,

Who, fram'd alone for tendernefs and love,

Some

Some two-fold game, perhaps, could better play, 110
Where nought occurr'd to lead her thoughts aftray.
Oft have I feen her with apparent fear
Cut in, reluctant, with her furly dear;
Who moft politely curs'd his wayward fate,
That then had fent him fuch a ftupid mate; 115
Nor thought that fault which now his temper crofs'd,
Was the beft virtue that a wife could boaft.
At firft the hufband peaceful meafures tries,
And warns her only with his hands and eyes;
Then gentle language—" Pray, my dear, take care—
" Do think a little—What have you put there?" 121
It rifes next to—" Play not then fo quick—
" The *trick* was mine—why did you trump my *trick*?"
Then, " Blefs me, girl, you're always going wrong—
" If thus you play, we cannot ftand it long." 125
And laft of all, while ftarting up, he cries,
" Death, hell, and fury! has the b—— no eyes?"
    Reverfe the picture now, and view the ftrife
Of henpeck'd hufband, and imperious wife.

L

Her

Here not by flow degrees the tempeft grows,       130
But burfts at once, and like a whirlwind blows ;
While the poor, timid, meek, domeftic thing
Runs cow'ring off, and hangs his flagging wing.

   No proof, perhaps, fo much can temper try,
As that which gaming's eager hours fupply ;       135
And therefore none, with thofe whofe beft regard
They wifh to keep, fhould ever touch a card :
But chief, ye melting maids, whofe conftant care
Spreads out for man the matrimonial fnare,
Left ye your temper's fecret faults betray,       140
At Whift but feldom with your lovers play :
Take timely warning from Smilinda's fate,
Whofe haplefs ftory I fhall now relate ;
For truth's beft habit is a pleafing tale,
And oft example moves where precepts fail.       145
   Pufillo now had reach'd the prime of life,
And long had look'd about to find a wife :
Small was his fize, but ample was his ftore,
And ampler ftill the character he bore.

                                        What

What wonder then that ev'ry prudent maid        150
With fecret joy his entrance ftill furvey'd ;
And tried unwearied ftill each female art,
To gain an int'reft in the pigmy's heart ?
But young Smilinda was the deftin'd fair
To prove the fweets of his peculiar care :        155
Her form was caft in that enchanting mould
Which love with moft delight will ftill behold ;
And fmiles complacent, with eternal grace,
Illum'd the fweetnefs of her angel face.
" Unmingled blifs (if fuch on earth there be)        160
" Muft fure, fair virgin, be to live with thee."
Such the conclufion which, at ev'ry view,
From her foft eyes the fond Pufillo drew.
And yet fufpicion kept his hopes in awe,
Nor could he wholly truft to what he faw.        165
He knew that ftill before the lover's eyes
The fimpleft beauty wears a flight difguife ;
And, ere he ventur'd boldly to demand
The rich donation of her virgin hand ;

To

To which, from many figns, he well could fee    170
That neither fhe nor hers averfe would be ;
He thought it beft fome farther care to take,
And one more nice experiment to make ;
By which he might the certain knowledge gain,
If fhe her temper could at cards retain :    175
Refolv'd that, if fhe well this trial bore,
He then would vainly hefitate no more ;
Would freely then declare his nuptial view,
And bid fufpicion and diftruft adieu.

  For this, occafion foon the pow'r fupplied,    180
And plac'd him oppofite his deftin'd bride,
One vernal ev'ning, in an eafy way,
A fingle rubber's length at Whift to play :
While coufin Booby's fon, a country 'fquire,
And aunt Rebecca made the fecond pair.    185

  But ere the firft commencing game was won,
Our artful lover had his fchemes begun ;
Some flight miftakes he had already made,
And then with anxious gaze her eyes furvey'd :

But

But ftill thofe eyes their placid charm retain,       190
And all her features ftill unmov'd remain ;
A peace that div'd no deeper than the fkin,
For fierce contending paffions rag'd within ;
Some fad wrong word was oft upon her tongue,
Came to the tip, and there a moment hung ;       195
But when reflection darted thro' her brain,
She gave a gulp—and down it went again.

   Nor was the conteft long, till each could claim
The fruitlefs triumph of a double game :
Thus far did chance her equal fmiles divide ;   200 ⎫
And ftill fhe feem'd unwilling to decide,            ⎬
Or give pre-eminence to either fide ;               ⎭
For, in the clofing game, they both at once
Within one ftep of conqueft's goal advance :
And now Pufillo thought the time was nigh,       205
The utmoft fuff'rance of her foul to try ;
For then each heart with greater zeal proceeds,
And each occurrence more emotion breeds ;

L 3

Nor

Nor did he grudge (to gain his curious views)

The rubber's praife and profit both to lofe.          210

 Smilinda now divides the cards with grace,

And Scotia's curfe difplays his nine-ey'd face;

" Diamonds again !" cried all that form'd the ring;

" I think we feldom have another thing."

The 'fquire leads clubs, and aunt Rebecca's queen 215

Retires in triumph from the level green :

But when fhe tried the fuit another round,

Fate was not then fo favourable found ;

For fcarce had Booby's king difplay'd his face,

Ere feiz'd and butcher'd by Pufillo's ace.          220

And now Pufillo's Pam, the prince of Loo,

In broad and brazen beauty meets the view :

To him on either hand fmall clubs are play'd,

While his renouncing partner drops a fpade :

Than try the ten he could not now do lefs,          225

And fortune crown'd his hopes with full fuccefs;

And from the trumps drew forth Rebecca's eight,

But from Smilinda's nine to meet its fate.

         She

She now with careful eye her hand furveys,

And from the knave a heart unwilling plays ; 230

A vile, unlucky lead in ev'ry view—

(And yet what better could the virgin do ?

Her king of fpades but once defended lay,

And could not to the ace be left a prey :

Her trumps, the laft refort, were now too few, 235

Since one from four her former triumph drew)

A vile, unlucky lead ; for full command

Lay couch'd in ambufh in Rebecca's hand.

Pufillo's king now fhows his honeft face,

A haplefs victim to her cruel ace : 240

And now Rebecca's queen a trick to gain

Had fanguine hopes ; nor did fhe hope in vain.

The lead fhould ne'er be chang'd without a caufe * ;

So from her hand another heart fhe draws.

* There is nothing more pernicious at the game of Whift, than to change fuits often, becaufe in every new fuit you run the rifk of giving your adverfary the tenace.

HOYLE, chap. xii.

L 4

Th s

This trick from fair Smilinda's lucklefs knave   245
Young Booby's deuce of trumps fuffic'd to fave.
And now another fuit, the fpades, he tries,
And views his partner's ace with joyful eyes:
The lead's return Smilinda's monarch drew—
'Twas both his int'reft, and his duty too.   250
But now the nymph no longer would delay,
Tho' rather weak, her fuit of trumps to play:
But here her partner lent her pow'rful aid,
By whofe good king the doubtful trick was made;
And fo next round fhe thought it no difgrace,   255
That her own queen fhould fall to Booby's ace.
The fov'reign pow'r fhe now at length had gain'd,
For tho' the queen was loft, the knave remain'd:
And now a lady rais'd to full command,
The queen of fpades, appear'd from Booby's hand. 260
With but two fpades Pufillo's hand begun,
And fix of trumps might now the trick have won;
(Three trumps were yet furvivors after all,
For poer Rebecca flinch'd the fecond call)

                                 And,

And, had he fo inclin'd, his chance was fure    265
This trick to conquer, and the game fecure;
Since Booby's ten, the laft concluding round,
Would from Smilinda's knave its fate have found.
But thoughts of diff'rent hue his mind engrofs;
His am'rous heart contemns the rubber's lofs;   270
With wilful error flips the trump to play,
And throws at one rafh ftroke their all away.

But when the falling cards the veil withdrew,
Which hid the groffnefs of his fault from view,
The gentle creature could endure no more,    275
She ftarted up, fhe ftamp'd, fhe rag'd, fhe fwore;
Proclaim'd her wrongs, and threw the cards away,
Nor longer in his prefence deign'd to ftay.

A work, alone by length of ages done,
Is oft by ruin in an hour undone;           280
And thus that flame, which had for years endur'd,
In one fhort minute was entirely cur'd:
No longer now the youth attentive paid
His daily vifits to the charming maid,
Who found, too late, fhe had herfelf betray'd; 285

And

And ev'ry female art effay'd in vain,
Her former empire o'er his heart to gain.

  At laſt, with hopes refulting from defpair,
She fate her down, to vent her cruel care;
While anxious fear fuppreſt her virgin pride,     290
And all the eloquence of love fupplied.
She firſt befought him for fweet pity's fake
No longer to refent the rude miſtake,
Which paſſion's pow'r had forc'd her once to make;
And next in bluſhing words ſhe let him know     295
How much his abfence fill'd her breaſt with woe;
With what affection and efteem combin'd
She view'd his perfon, and beheld his mind;
And ſhould his boſom feel an equal care,
She hinted, that he might his foul declare,     300
And need not of a juſt return defpair.
Such was the fcope on which her fyren tongue
Full many a note of foft allurement fung;
Concluding thus: that tho' they both were
     young,

It was not right in ufelefs, vain delay          305
To wafte the prime of life's uncertain day.

    With trembling hope fhe fent the billet ftrait,
Whofe doubtful iffue was to fix her fate;
Nor for an anfwer had fhe long to wait:
Th' important note a yellow wafer feal'd,          310
'Twas brief, but yet his mind enough reveal'd:
" When cards and dice are banifh'd from the land,
" Pufillo then will afk Smilinda's hand."

IN order that the defcription of a hand at Whift, which has been attempted in this Canto, may be the more eafily comprehended by the reader, I fhall fubjoin both a view of the different hands, and a fcheme of the cards in the order they were played.

### BOOBY'S, THE ELDER HAND.

Ace, ten, tray, and deuce of trumps—king and three fmall clubs—queen and two fmall fpades—two fmall hearts.

### PUSILLO'S, THE SECOND HAND.

King, fix, and four of trumps—ace, knave, ten, and a fmall club—king and three fmall hearts—two fmall fpades.

### REBECCA'S, THE THIRD HAND.

Eight and five of trumps—ace, knave, and three fmall fpades—ace, queen, and a fmall heart—queen and two fmall clubs.

### SMILINDA'S, THE LAST HAND.

Queen, knave, nine, and feven of trumps—knave and three fmall hearts—king and two fmall fpades—two fmall clubs.

### DIAMONDS ARE TRUMPS—AND THE NINE TURNED UP BY SMILINDA.

#### Round I.

Booby's deuce of clubs—Pufillo's tray—Rebecca's queen—and Smilinda's four.

Round

### Round II,

Rebecca's five of clubs—Smilinda's fix—Booby's king—and Pufillo's ace.

### Round III.

Pufillo's knave of clubs—Rebecca's feven—Smilinda's deuce of fpades—and Booby's eight of clubs.

### Round IV.

Pufillo's ten of clubs—Rebecca's eight of trumps—Smilinda's nine—and Booby's nine of clubs.

### Round V

Smilinda's deuce of hearts—Booby's tray—Pufillo's king—and Rebecca's ace.

### Round VI,

Rebecca's queen of hearts—Smilinda's four—Booby's five—and Pufillo's fix.

### Round VII.

Rebecca's feven of hearts—Smilinda's knave—Booby's deuce of trumps—and Pufillo's eight of hearts.

### Round VIII.

Booby's tray of fpades—Pufillo's four—Rebecca's ace—and Smilinda's five.

### Round IX.

Rebecca's fix of fpades—Smilinda's king—Booby's feven—and Pufillo's eight.

### Round X.

Smilinda's feven of trumps—Booby's tray—Pufillo's king—and Rebecca's five.

Round

### Round XI.

Pufillo's four of trumps—Rebecca's nine of fpades—Smilinda's queen of trumps—and **Booby's ace.**

### Round XII.

Booby's queen of fpades—Pufillo's **nine of hearts—Rebecca's** ten of fpades—and Smilinda's knave of **trumps.**

### Round XIII.

Smilinda's ten of hearts—Booby's ten of **trumps**—Pufillo's fix—and Rebecca's knave of fpades.

Smilinda three **tricks,** and Pufillo three—Booby three **tricks.** but Rebecca four.

# W H I S T.

## CANTO XI.

# ARGUMENT.

The Author's complaint againſt his Father; who obliges
him to clap to the end of his work, a Lecture againſt
Gaming, of his dictating.

We think our fathers fools, fo wife we grow.    POPE.

Difficilis, querulus, laudator temporis acti
Se puero, cenfor, caftigatorque minorum.    HORACE.

GOOD Lord! what arrant fools fome people are,
With all their ftuff of prudence, fenfe, and care!
In vain old father Time his influence tries;
He makes them proud, but never makes them wife.
They fondly think that they fhould all things know, 5
Becaufe they liv'd fome fifty years ago;
Nor once reflect, this age has other rules,
And other maxims than thefe formal fools.
Were it not grofsly to abufe my pow'r,
I could rail on, and curfe them by the hour:    10
For pure vexation I could almoft cry;
But liften, reader, and I'll tell you why.

A fire I have (fo much the worfe for me),
As great a pedant as you'd wifh to fee;

M                              Morofe

Morose, ill-natur'd, rigid, and severe ;     15
Sententious, dull, old-fashion'd, stiff, and queer :
In short, a soul that hates each custom new,
And censures all that youngsters like to do.
Those schemes of mine which have to him been
      shewn,
He seldom praises but in sneering tone,     20
And likes no wit or wisdom but his own.
Without his knowledge then I Whist began,
And still from him conceal'd the darling plan ;
For, ev'n without a proof, I could have guess'd
That such a project would not hit his taste.     25

  Now when thus far I had the strain pursued,
I paus'd, and what was done with joy review'd ;
And thought it (if I here the truth may tell)
Hit off upon the whole exceeding well,
And only wanting for a smart farewell.     30

  But whilst I thus indulg'd a poet's pride,
And fondly sail'd on fancy's golden tide,
I little thought Papa was at my side.

                              For

For his ſtern eyes I was but ill prepar'd,
And could have gladly then his viſit ſpar'd :    35
But vile, malignant chance would have it ſo,
And I with patience now muſt bear the blow.
—At once, with looks which dark ſuſpicion wore,
He from my trembling hand the papers tore,
And ran, with ſullen glance, the ſprightly pages
    o'er.    40

Ev'n thoſe I thought, while I purſued the toil,
That none could e'er peruſe without a ſmile,
Had not the pow'r his anger to beguile.
Unalter'd ſtill his awful face remain'd,
And all its native rigour ſtill retain'd :    45
Nay worſe ; a darker hue his front embrown'd,
Or (not to ſpeak in poetry) he frown'd.

    Thus thro' the work with haſty glance he ran,
And thus his ſtern, deſpotic ſpeech begàn :

    " So ſo, young graceleſs ; now your ſtuff is done,
" You think, no doubt, you have a triumph won ; 51
" You think, no doubt, that all is mighty fine,
" Wit, ſenſe, and elegance in ev'ry line ;

    " And

" And with a brazen front may mean to try

" In this fool's coat to meet the public eye.          55

" Audacious boy ! and could you then suppose

" That I would see you thus yourself expose ?

" That I would e'er permit a son of mine

" To future times such lessons to consign ?

" So widely thus from moral truth to stray,          60

" And poison thus in gilded pills convey ?

" But if, in reason's spite, you still persist

" To claim distinction as the Bard of Whist,

" I am resolv'd that this infected song

" Shall bear at least its antidote along ;          65

" And those who gaming's charms have heard from you,

" From me at least shall hear its horrors too."

With this last hint I was not quite displeas'd,

And quick as thought the fair occasion seiz'd ;

And promis'd strait, with some invective strong,

Against the love of play to close the song.          71

But here, alas ! the old suspicious Don

Was far too cunning for his sprightly son.

I

" No

" **No no**," he cried, " that plan could never do ;

" It is not by the help of fuch as you, 75

" That reafon's voice muft folly's pow'r fubdue."

" To me, young fir, refign that arduous **care,**

" And for the tafk of fcribe yourfelf prepare ;

" **While I** retire, thofe fcatter'd **thoughts** to find,

" With which the fubject oft has fill'd my mind ; 80

" To which at times I have attention paid,

" And oft with grief its rapid growth furvey'd,

" And when my hints are rang'd in juft array,

" I then will dictate what you **ought to** fay :"

So fpake the angry fire, and ftately ftalk'd away.

**Fain** would I, while he yet remain'd in fight, 86

**Have boldly urg'd** my juft, exclufive right

To manage as I chofe, and thought it fit

Th' unborrow'd offspring of my native **wit :**

But terror aw'd, and what I meant to fay 90

Stuck in my throat, and could not find a way.

Thus muft this tongue, by fancy's pow'r refin'd,

Be made the organ of another's mind ;

M 3 And

And thus, by cruelty before unknown,
Be forc'd to utter feelings not my own;                95
And thus my pretty work be fairly fpoil'd,
Becaufe I chance—to be my father's child.

  But hufh ! he comes again ; I hear the found
Of thofe grave fteps that fcatter fear around.
Now, reader, now, prepare your patient ear         100
A lecture dull of formal length to hear ;
But which, I truft, will never reach your brain,
But from your other ear come out again.

  But hold ; and, ere I write a fentence more,
Let me for that another leaf turn o'er.                105
You underftand me—for it would not do,
That he fhould liften* all I fpeak to you.

---

* As they had feen me, with thefe hangman's hands,
  Lift'ning their fear.
         SHAKESPEAR's MACBETH, Act 2, Sc. 3.

# WHIST.

## CANTO XII.

## ARGUMENT.

Serious lecture againft gaming.—Hiftory of a fkilful and fortunate gamefter.—Poftfcript by the Author in the humorous ftyle.

Arm'd at all points, to fight that hydra, Gaming.    MOORE.

————Contra o veneno urgente,
He tido por antidoto excellente.    CAMOENS.

OF all the plagues that from the birth of time
Have rang'd by turns this sublunary clime,
And in their various forms the nations curs'd,
The boundless love of play is sure the worst.
Not that disease, whose once resistless pow'r     5
With envious malice blasted beauty's flow'r;
Which from the east with those weak fools re-
　　　turn'd,
Whose frantic breasts with bigot fury burn'd:
Nor that commission'd by the pow'rs above,
With tortures just to punish lawless love:     10
　　　　　　　　　　　　　　　　That

That cruel fcourge*, which from the weftern fhore
To Europe's coaft the Spanifh robbers bore,
Such havock fpreads, as on his baleful wings
The univerfal pow'r of gaming brings;
That pow'r which now pervades each tainted foul,
And fcatters death from Indus to the Pole;          16
From where remote, on Tonquin's golden fhore,
The tawny crew the pow'rs of chance adore;
And, when refources fail, no fcruple make
Their weeping children or their wives to ftake;     20
To where at home, in this degen'rate land,
In ev'ry ftreet the fanes of ruin ftand;
Where fraud's pernicious band, unwearied ftill,
Invoke the demons of unlawful fkill:
That felfifh pow'r, the foe of ufeful art,          25
Which moft can harden and contract the heart;

* Il eft certain, que ce venin qui empoifonne les fources de la
Vie, était propre de l'Amérique——et aujourd'hui, après un moment paffé et oublié depuis des années, la plus chafte union peut
être fuivie du plus cruel et du plus honteux des fléaux, dont le
genre humain foit affligé.

VOLTAIRE, ESSAI SUR L'HIST. GEN. t. iii, ch. 37.

Which

Which keeps in floth* the outward frame confin'd,
And but to vicious action fpurs the mind ;
That pow'r whofe growth I can with grief forefee
Some future day will Europe's ruin be.              30

But words that feek our paffions to reftrain,
In this light age of folly's boundlefs reign,
But fmall attention can expect to gain ;
And it perhaps were better now to try
What ftronger aids example can fupply.              35

A man there was (if public fame fay true),
The firft and luckieft of the gaming crew;
A fplendid fortune who refolv'd to gain,
Without corporeal labour's tirefome pain,
Or mental efforts of the ftudious brain.            40

---

* Surely that vice deferves the keeneft invective, which, more
than any other, has a natural and invincible tendency to narrow
and to harden the heart, by impreffing and keeping up habits of
felfifhnefs. " I forefee" (faid Montefquieu to a friend vifiting
him at La Brede) " that gaming will one day be the ruin of Eu-
" rope.—During play, the body is in a ftate of indolence, and
" the mind in a ftate of vicious activity."

WARTON's ESSAY ON POPE, Sect. x. 18.

For this, to gaming's art he kept confin'd

The whole attention of his anxious mind ;

For this, in trying various modes of play,

He fpent for years the folitary day ;

For this, on flighteft food he chofe to dine,          45

Nor e'er would tafte intoxicating wine ;

That nought might thus obfcure his mental fight,

Or blaft the hopes of each triumphant night.

And thus at length a height of fkill he gain'd,

Which fcarce one mortal had before attain'd ;          50

And thus at length amafs'd an ampler ftore

Than ever had been thus amafs'd before.

What tho', perhaps, fome widow'd mother's tongue

Might curfe the fource from which her forrow
    fprung ;

Might curfe that fkill which drove, with cruel hand,

Her ruin'd fon to quit his native land :          56

What tho', perhaps, fome orphan weak and pale,

With hunger faint, and fhiv'ring in the gale,

                                 Might

Might on that chariot fix his weeping eye,

In guilty fplendor as it glitter'd by, 60

Which bore the wretch, who from his father tore

Without remorfe his patrimonial ftore;

Who charg'd his foul with fhame's defpairing
weight,

And drove him headlong from the brink of fate:

Yet would that chariot all obftruction fpurn, 65

And not lefs rapid to the dome return,

Which, rear'd in Scotia's land, may ftill be found,

And cumbers with its weight the groaning ground;

Which, as it there in hateful fplendor ftands,

With daring hopes the gamefter's heart expands; 70

While reafon's fober eye beholds it ftill,

The fhameful monument of guilty fkill.

Oh that, when firft he view'd the finifh'd toil,

And gaz'd with triumph on the fplendid pile,

Some demon then, or fome avenging god, 75

Had touch'd the ftructure with his pow'rful rod,

And

And made it sink before his startled eyes,

Like card-built fabrics, never more to rise.

How would the wretch have shrunk with sudden
    awe,

And quak'd with terror, when amaz'd he saw,   80

Instead of arches, gates, and colonnades,

A heap of clubs and diamonds, hearts and spades!

'Tis true indeed, that few or none complain'd,

That what they lost had been unfairly gain'd:

But how can this his character excuse,       85

Or make his life its guilty colour lose?

As well might he, who lurks beside the way,

To make th' unwary traveller his prey;

With pistols arm'd, and constant practice bold,

Who stops th' unarm'd, the timid, and the old;  90

Proclaims his wants, and asks a quick supply,

Which if they give not, they are sure to die—

As well this wretch, when talking with his friend,

Might fair and open dealing recommend;

For

For meaner rogues a juſt abhorrence feel, 95
And blefs his Maker that he did not ſteal.

But in its juſt revenge tho'. Heav'n be ſlow,
It will not always let the ſinner go ;
For now, to cloſe the ſcene, his worſt of foes,
Conſcience herſelf, in awful fury roſe, 100
Refum'd at laſt her long-neglected pow'r,
And ſtung with painful thought each tort'ring
    hour.——
She brought reflection's band in dark array,
To cloud the light of ev'ry cheerlefs day ;
And fill'd with ghaſtly phantoms of affright 105
The weary length of ev'ry trembling night.
Nor did ſhe once remit her cruel rage,
Until ſhe drove him from the mortal ſtage,
To thoſe abodes, where he perhaps ſhall find
That man for diff'rent duties was defign'd, 110
And form'd for ſcience of another kind,
Than in the vain purſuits of worthleſs play
To waſte the precious hours of life away :

Perhaps

Perhaps to dwell in that appointed place
Of pain and grief, of horror and difgrace,          115
Where He refides, whofe books (to fraud fo dear)
With fuch unwearied pains he ftudied here.

---

# POSTSCRIPT.

NOW, bleft be Heav'n, the tedious lecture's o'er,
And old Square-toes will trouble us no more;
And yet I cannot leave you thus behind,          120
With fuch abfurd impreffions on your mind,
Nor wholly thus to his advice refign,
Until you hear a little more of mine.

Can there then be whofe tempers are fo rough,
Whofe hearts are made of fuch unfeeling ftuff,          125
That they could wifh from our imperfect life
To cut the brilliant hours of painted ftrife,

And

And from the worthlefs world to drive away
The hopes, the pleafures, and the pains of play ?
Let thofe who harbour fuch a ftrange defire,        130
To fome obfcure, fequefter'd nook **retire ;**
Where thro' the **tedious year no Spades** are found,
But thofe that ferve to penetrate the ground ;
No Clubs, but thofe, with which fome angry clown
Knocks, at a time, his fellow ruftic down ;        135
No Hearts, but thofe, with which in paffion's hour
The wanton boy difplays his fovereign pow'r :
And as for Diamonds, you in vain may call,
For there they never can be found at all.
There let all fuch their lives in languor wafte,        140
And rail at pleafures which they cannot tafte.

But ye that live in fafhion's polifh'd climes,
In this great art inftruct your fons **betimes ;**
Let this be ftill the firft of your regards,
Before their letters let them learn their cards.        145
Nor do I yet defpair to fee the day,
When hoftile armies rang'd in neat array,
Inftead of fighting, fhall engage in play ;

N

When

When peaceful Whift the quarrel fhall decide,
And Chriftian blood be fpilt on neither fide. 150
Then duels too, or any other fray,
Might all be fought in this good harmlefs way;
Then pleas no more fhould wait the tardy laws,
But one odd *trick* at once conclude the caufe.
Tho' fome will fay that this is nothing new, 155
For here there have been long *odd tricks* enow.

    Thus Britain ftill, to all the world's furprife,
In this great fcience fhall progreffive rife,
Till ages hence, when all of each degree
Shall play the game as well as Hoyle or me. 160

## THE END.

As an antidote to the poifonous doctrine delivered with
regard to matrimony in the feventh Canto*, the Author begs leave to fubjoin here a Sonnet written upon
the fame fubject, which will fhew how very different are
his real fentiments from thofe of the character he has
chofen to affume.

# S O N N E T.

HOW bleft is he, however low his ftate,
   To whom the bounty of indulgent Heav'n
A tender, conftant, kind congenial mate,
   To fhare his pleafures and his pains, has giv'n!

To her fecure he opens all his heart,
   Nor knows one thought he wifhes to conceal;
Fearlefs to her can ev'ry care impart,
   And all the forrows of his foul reveal.

Tho' all abroad refufe his fpirit reft,
   Tho' fortune frowns, and friends may prove
      unkind;
At home, he knows, remains one faithful breaft,
   Where ftill his weary head repofe fhall find.

Ah! why to me does fate fuch blifs deny,
And doom me ftill to live " a folitary fly?"

V. 105—108.

www.ingramcontent.com/pod-product-compliance
Lightning Source LLC
Chambersburg PA
CBHW031104020726
47495CB00007B/2034